MW01140029

MURDER SAUCE

© 2017 Marcus V. Calvert

By Tales Unlimited, LLC.

For permissions, contact:
https://squareup.com/store/TANSOM.

Cover by Lincoln Adams

Edited by Ed Buchanan

ACKNOWLEDGEMENTS

I'd like to thank Ed Buchanan (my editor) for his expertise, steady support, and blunt-force candor.

I'd also like to thank Lincoln Adams (my cover artist) for his time, patience, and wicked-awesome skill.

Rose, thanks for keeping me in the game.

To everyone else who had a hand in this twisted thing being written (living or not), I thank you.

I must also tip a hat to my fellow artists and strangers-turned-fans. You truly are a hip crowd.

CHAPTER ONE

With a trusting smile, I slowly reached out with both hands.

"Try again, hun," I gently prodded.

"How far should I go?" Lia Falsham asked.

"Show me what happens tomorrow," I replied.

Lia looked up with a quiet frustration. This time, the sixteen-year-old precog didn't fake a smile. She merely placed her smaller hands into mine, closed her eyes, and attempted to show me my future.

Seconds passed . . . and nothing happened. With a defeated shrug, Lia stepped back. I did what I always did—pulled her in and gave her a hug. After her parents were gunned down, Lia became my daughter in all ways but blood. I knew how much this power meant to her. Yet, while I'd never admit it, I was kinda glad it was gone.

Precognition was more of a curse than a blessing. Had Lia been born a typical precog, her visions would've been unreliable glimpses of the future. Over time, this power could erode a precog's sanity, turning him/her into a babbling head case. What made Lia special was that she was born with psychic safeguards.

Six months ago, the former precog could've asked a question about my future, touched me, and I'd see the answer. Her visions were always detailed and perfectly accurate. The main drawback to Lia's power was that it only worked once per day per person (another safeguard). Still, since Lia outsourced her power, it didn't bother her mind at all.

When she was one of my mercs, we called her "Forecast." Like a psychic weather girl, her visions saved plenty of lives—including my own. At 5'6", Lia was almost as tall as me. She got her height from her dad. Her green eyes, short black hair, and freckled beauty came from her mom.

"Sorry, Dad."

"No apologies," I replied, still locked in our embrace.

We were both sweaty from yet another round of unarmed sparring on a large red training mat. As I was teaching her every dirty trick I knew, Lia helped me get my moves back. Eleven years as a fixer left me a bit rusty (and overweight).

In the light, the kid was faster than me and fought twice as dirty. In darkness, when my powers still worked, she couldn't touch me. I noticed the deepening shadows as they rolled across the hardwood floor. Night approached.

"It's almost time," Lia said, her eyes following my gaze.

"I'll fix dinner."

"*Hot Pockets* again?" Lia groaned.

"It beats fighting crime with your chili in my guts," I muttered with a half-glance her way.

"That was not my fault," she replied with a defensive grin. "Some crime fighters have weaker stomachs than others."

With that, Lia grabbed her towel and headed for the guest room (now hers). I grinned as I headed for the main bathroom and hopped in the shower. This property was the only one I had left (officially, anyway). When the mobs seized my assets, they let the cops come in and loot the place. Luckily, I didn't keep any contraband here—just $30 million in walking around cash. The cops cracked all three of my hidden safes and stole everything but the fucking soap.

Assuming I made it back that night, I was supposed to be demoralized or something. Instead, I turned the empty space into a private dojo and personally handled

Lia's training. Oh, and someone (not me, of course) put Police Commissioner Harris' face through the windshield of his new Mercedes.

But again . . . it wasn't me.

After a quick shower, I grabbed a razor and trimmed my brownish-gray goatee. With a towel around my waist, I looked like a rock-hard athlete. Hard to believe that I had to die to get this ripped. Six months ago, I was Benjamin Cly—merchant of evil. The shadow mutation turned my excess fat into muscle, which became superhumanly strong in the absence of light.

I still needed a tan, though.

My wet, graying hair was slicked back and recently trimmed. As usual, my surgically altered face was butt-ugly and finally showing the wrinkles of my forty-three years. Only now, with the physique and all, I didn't have to pay for sex anymore. Stranger still was the fact that I was in a serious relationship. Juanita and I had been together for almost two months. Things were fun, monogamous, and flat-out kinky.

It was funny how my life had switched gears.

I didn't want to fight crime. It was the price I paid for putting Seamus O'Flernan in the ground. Even after losing my criminal empire, I didn't regret his death. The old man was a charming piece of shit with way too many enemies.

I just had the rotten luck of being his last one.

Based on proof that I had just cause, the mobs showed me "mercy" in the form of Community Service. The decades-old penalty was created by Seamus himself to deal with influential crooks who couldn't be killed outright. I easily fit the bill.

As a fixer, I once ran a stable of high-end mercenary talent with clients all over the globe. Name the job and I'd see it done for a wicked fee. My people worked miracles on any side of the law, either saving and/or killing thousands without a qualm. Interpol once ranked me as the eighth most dangerous man on the planet.

Had the mobs chosen to kill me that night, one/many of my mercs might've retaliated. When the mobs forced me to accept Community Service, I had (in essence) renounced my criminal status in Pillar City. I had to shut down my firm and fire my mercs. The mobs confiscated my (traceable) wealth, hired away some of my top mercs, and forced me to start from scratch.

Then, to add insult to injury, they imposed a few more terms on my Community Service. I couldn't engage in criminal acts. Anyone who worked with me could be killed outright. If I left town, I would've been hunted down. And every night (for the rest of my life), I had to personally fight crime without infringing on mob operations. Violating any of these terms would result in my ending up dead really fast.

By accepting the yoke of Community Service, the four mobs—especially the O'Flernans—couldn't touch me. That was the only silver lining to this shitty arrangement. Of course, that didn't stop the Irish fuckers. Instead of sending their own soldiers to kill me, they simply put a massive kill bounty on my head.

Luckily, no one knew that I had super powers. They looked at me and saw a fat guy in a suit. Everyone expected to read about my gruesome death within a week.

That was over five months ago.

In the interest of self-preservation, I honored my end of the agreement. Still, anyone who knew Pillar City—really knew it—would admit that its streets couldn't be tamed. This town was so brilliantly corrupt that Afghan warlords sent their kids here to become better criminals!

Yet, here I was . . . keeping the streets "safe."

Of course, I wasn't planning on simply fighting crime like a good little peon. My initial idea was to turn my Community Service status into a business venture. Even a crime fighter could make money on these streets. Yet, with the heroes dead and genocidal maniacs coming out of the woodwork, I had to indefinitely shelve those plans.

All I've really had time to do was eat, sleep, and save the fucking day. I've actually saved the world five times now. The Chinese, Colombian, and Russian mobs were (reluctantly) cheering me on from the sidelines. While the Irish canceled the kill bounty, they still wanted me dead. Add to that the growing line of new enemies I was making and I figured I wasn't going to live a long and fruitful life. Too stupid to run, I played my hand with every intention of winning . . . even though I couldn't.

What sucked the most was that the low-end crime in this town just kept on coming (stuff that shocked even me). Being an unreformed crook at heart, I shouldn't mind the decadent delights of this place. Yet, with every depraved crime scene I found or every sick bastard I put down, I grew more disgusted with Pillar City.

I finished my shave, toweled off, and put on my working clothes.

The black silk boxers and matching socks went on first. I then put on the ArgoKnight-issue flight collar. Dull gray and tougher than steel, I wore it around my neck like the good luck charm it was. Then came the black pants and work boots. The same went for my thick, black turtleneck sweater. I left the woolen overcoat on the bed.

Except for my underwear, this "costume" of mine was fully laced with bullet- and heat-resistant materials. Even when I could still regenerate, I had a healthy respect for body armor. With the weather warming up, I had summer wear on order (something the comic books never seemed to mention when I was a kid).

I slipped on my thick brown gun belt, which came with empty pouches and three holsters. It even had a few gadgets sewn into the leather. Holstered in its left side was a Colt Peacemaker. The .45-caliber revolver was actually more of a miniature grenade launcher. Made out of hyper-alloy metals, it came with a built-in taser in the butt.

Also, the "bullets" were miniature smart warheads. Dubbed "Embedder" rounds, the slugs were designed to only arm when fired through this gun. Each shot could punch through five inches of steel. If an Embedder round hit something harder than that, it would flatten and self-adhere to the target (like old gum). Either way, after a five-count, the slug would explode with enough force to level a small house.

I had two spare reloads tucked into my clothing. The gun was already cleaned and loaded but I checked it again. For the more conventional threats, I holstered a pair of Glock .45's to the back of the gun belt. Two spare clips were already tucked away in my coat.

Then I put on my black gloves and scarf/mask. Right now, the black scarf covered my head like a pirate-style doo rag. When needed, it would cover my face and neck with its thin, see-through fabric. It even came with a built-in air filter. I looked around for my sensor goggles and found them under the bed (again).

After I slipped them over my mask, the internal display fired up. While they looked like a black pair of welder goggles, these puppies had repeatedly saved my life over the last six months. They could detect the presence of hostiles, threats, or victims. With my shadow mutation half-cured, my heightened senses were all but gone. These babies picked up the slack.

Once the goggles were set, I grabbed my radio. The device rested in a red metal case, which was plugged into a wall charger. I pulled the thin, transparent piece of plastic out and slipped it over my upper teeth. To the untrained eye, it could've been mistaken as one of those mouthpieces that boxers wore. With the radio in my mouth, it was less likely to get broken or lost. Should someone ever catch me, my captors might overlook it.

I pulled the utility harness/scabbard off a door hook and fastened it. Thirty-six tiny gadgets were tucked into this gray metal sash, which ran diagonally across my chest. On the back was a black scabbard with my wakizashi sheathed inside. The razor-sharp, nigh-unbreakable weapon was the 29-inch version of a katana.

Once I put the black overcoat on, I loaded my pockets with the usual: Zippo lighter, a pack of Marlboros, three grand worth of petty cash, two small burner phones, a pouch of untraceable diamonds (street value about $2.12 million), keys, two black pens, and a pack of condoms (for luck). I stepped out into the living room to find Lia in jeans and a purple sweater. She was mopping the training mat like she did every night.

"Wanna come with?" I offered.

Lia looked up with a surprised smile. Cooped up in this building, surrounded with bodyguards, she did nothing but train. The city's "fresh" air would do her some good, even with the risks involved.

Besides, her armor was collecting dust, which wasn't healthy.

*   *   *

We stepped into her neat bedroom and knocked seven times on the inside of her door. At the foot of her king-sized bed, the hardwood floor slid open. Up rose Lia's armor. Naturally, it was designed and constructed by Samir. The surly old "tailor" had designed the best armor suits on the planet. Once I paid him $2 billion up front, I gave him a grocery list of the features. When her suit was done, Samir admitted that he was proud (and a little scared) of his creation.

Under the gleaming light, the medieval-style armor was a mix of silvery chain mail and dark-blue plate. It would've been a perfect addition to any museum's armor exhibit. The overlapping plates were harder than diamond and lighter than plastic, as was the chainmail.

Typical medieval armor came in pieces and took forever to put on. Mounted on a pole stand, Lia's armor was designed as a one-piece outfit. The back end opened and Lia simply stepped inside. The armor closed around her from the ankle boots to the chainmail hood. The visor's eye slits flashed a bright red for a moment and then a soft hum emanated from the suit. Miniature clicking noises indicated a system diagnostic.

"Comfy?" I asked.

"I'm good," Lia replied through her armor's voice synthesizer. Anyone hearing her speak would think there was a mature woman inside.

The armor, with Lady Justice engraved on the chest, went silent.

"Systems green," Lia announced as she stepped away from the stand and clenched her fists. "Wanna spar now?"

"Hell no," I grinned. "Let's fight some crime."

"Ready when you are," she replied, sounding juiced to the gills with anticipation.

Lia stepped passed me. Her armor's tread was quieter than mine. I loudly cleared my throat before she made it to the door. Lia stopped and turned my way, assuming that she had forgotten something. I casually slipped my right arm around my daughter's thick armored waist and walked her out of the room.

"You're forgetting the First Rule of Crime Fighting," I scolded her.

"Ahh," she chuckled. "'Never fight crime on an empty stomach,'"

"Damn skippy," I replied.

CHAPTER TWO

We were out of *Hot Pockets* but there was plenty of cold cereal and fresh fruit in the fridge. The sun was down by the time we started eating. Lia's visor slid open to expose her face as she dined.

There wasn't much chitchat.

If anything, I wondered if Lia needed a pep talk. When her precog was intact, she could've shown me exactly how tonight would turn out. Then we'd figure out whether to change that future or go along with it. Without her power, the kid had to be nervous—armor be damned.

This was my fault.

Before I died, I could touch any superhuman and steal his/her/its power(s). The effect was temporary but useful. A "gift" from my black ops days, the lab-given genetic augmentation had a shelf life of twenty years. After that, my organs were supposed to fail and kill me.

That was twenty-two years ago.

At the ten-year mark, I grew tired of "public sector" work and faked my death. By the time I became a fixer, I had a new name, face, and even skin color. To truly stay under the radar, I had to stop using my power ripping ability. The genetic inactivity bought me those two extra years . . . until last October when some assholes tried to destroy Pillar City.

To stop that catastrophe, I taxed my power beyond its waning limits. Needing every tactical edge, I ripped Lia's power and then gave her a vision. It allowed her to shoot one of my former mercs right before he could lob a stun grenade our way. If that grenade had gone off, over two million people—including Lia—would be dead right now.

Too bad her power hasn't returned.

I called in Teke the next day. The cagey old telepath went over her psyche and concluded that my actions had "broken" her power. To undo the damage, Teke tried every bit of psi-therapy. In the end, nothing worked. Fortunately, I didn't raise Lia to be helpless.

My mercs had trained Lia since she was five. Through them, she picked up enough diverse skills to join any spec ops unit. Comfortable growing up with killers, she took it all in like it was a fun little game. On that fateful October night, Lia reflexively fell back on her training . . . and learned what it was like to kill someone.

Lia actually handled it pretty well. She was sad for a week or two. After that, she seemed herself again. I could tell that it still bothered her, though. That's why I had Samir throw in all kinds of non-lethal weaponry when he built her armor. Odds were that (even with the armor) Lia would have to kill again someday. My hope was that she wouldn't hesitate when the time came.

We stepped into my private elevator, which I installed when I bought the building. In my possession for some eight years, the twelve-story structure was home. On the outside, it looked like a refurbished 20's-era office building with a rectangular design and concrete facade.

Inside were twenty-three luxury lofts (two to a floor). My loft took up the entire seventh floor. When I was a fixer, I had a tenant in every loft. Now, I had them emptied as a security precaution.

I punched in the eight-digit code into the elevator's keypad.

"I almost forgot to ask," I smiled. "You want to be the sidekick? Or should I?"

"You're Robin tonight," Lia replied.

That's my girl.

I pressed the emergency stop button and the floor fell out. Lia managed (this time) not to squeal with childish delight as we fell. The elevator floor slid closed above us. Sensors in the elevator car scanned us. If we didn't check out, the tractor beams (hidden at the bottom of the shaft) wouldn't kick in and we'd have to deal with gravity's cruel whims.

Invisible beams slowed us down around the fifth floor and gently lowered us to the bottom. A hidden section of wall opened, leading to my new lair. Six months ago, it was merely a safe room (my largest). Now, it was tricked out with weapons, computers, a mini-lab, and its own exit tunnel. Damned thing even had vending machines—because I'm badassed that way.

The main computer activated, along with everything else. Grace Lexia's face appeared on the screen. Coffee in hand, the psi-hacker had been running ragged. While she was forty-six, Grace looked a half-decade younger. On second glance, I spotted some new gray strands in her frizzy brown hair. Tied up in a ponytail, it accentuated her plain black T-shirt and decent rack. She didn't bother with makeup (and didn't need it). In the background was a dimly lit brick wall.

The one-time Pillar City cop quit after her former colleagues blew up her house—with her in it. The trauma activated a latent psychic ability known as psi-hacking. Basically, Grace could control any computer she could interface with either via Wi-Fi or direct physical contact.

Psi-hackers still had to bypass encryptions to take over a computer. Luckily for us, Grace was one of the best. The gal could simultaneously hack through thousands of high-end firewalls within minutes. Were it not for her goodie-two-shoes mindset, her level of skill would've frightened even me.

While I wouldn't want to admit this, Grace was one of the few super heroes left in this world. She didn't wear tights or fly around. The psi-hacker simply prowled the Internet, looking for potential catastrophes. Then she'd warn the right people, agencies, and/or news outlets. When Grace Lexia warned someone, they tended to listen—or die. Her indirect approach had saved the world maybe . . . hundreds of times over the last ten years.

These days, when her methods didn't work, she'd send me.

"Morning, Grace," I nodded.

The psi-hacker frowned and asked, "How do you know it's not night here?"

"Because you're a sucker for Europe," I replied. "Something about 'the food being better,' if memory serves."

Grace gave me an enigmatic shrug and then smiled at Lia.

"Taking the new armor out for a field run?" Grace asked.

"Yep," Lia replied. "I get to be the Green Hornet. Cly's my Kato."

Grace's left eyebrow went up.

"That'll make headlines tomorrow," she muttered. "What's your codename gonna be?"

"What's wrong with Forecast?" Lia innocently asked.

"Nothing," I scoffed, "unless you want to remind everyone that you're my kid."

Lia sighed through her armor.

Yes, I kept her off the grid as long as possible. Once my firm crumbled, word got out about Lia and her ability to predict the future. That she was my adopted daughter, and thus, my only real vulnerability. Some would want access to her power. Others would use her to get to me. All of this annoyed her to no end.

"Frankly, it's probably smarter to just go anonymous," Grace said. "Let some media schmuck name you."

"Maybe you're right," Lia replied. "Besides, my old handle doesn't apply anymore."

"It doesn't go with the armor either," I grinned.

"What about you, Dad?" she asked. "Shouldn't you have a fancy codename?"

"My name's scary enough," I replied with a cold grin.

"That's for damned sure," Grace smirked.

"What's the crime like tonight?" I asked, shifting the conversation.

Grace paused to take it all in. Before I went out, the psi-hacker would tip me off to any juicy crimes, events, and/or potentially bad things in the area. The ex-cop in her wanted to clean up Pillar City so much. The realist in her knew better than to try.

"The city's jumping for a Tuesday," Grace reported. "Street crimes are up 13%."

"Anything in common?" Lia asked.

"Nah," Grace replied with a familiar disgust.

"And yet our official crime rate's so low," Lia mocked.

I grinned. Pillar City's crime rate probably rivaled any Third World shithole. The only difference was that we kept our sins quiet. It was good for business, tourism, and long-term criminal growth. Anyone trying to accurately report on this city's crime scene ended up taking a bribe or a bullet. I should know–I arranged both in my fixer days.

I tapped my dental radio with the tip of my tongue.

"How's my signal?" I asked.

"Five-by-five," Grace replied. "Full audio-visual. Tracking signal's encrypted. How are you for gadgets?"

"Running a bit light," I replied.

"Gunrack's got a fresh batch waiting for you," Grace said. "Try to make it last a few weeks, huh?"

"Hey," I shrugged, "justice ain't easy."

Grace sipped her coffee with a shake of her head. Easily worth billions, the psi-hacker had financed her operations—and ours—by ripping money from bad guys. The funny thing about her thefts was that some of her victims hadn't figured out that they were broke yet.

"What about your insides?" Grace asked.

I rolled my eyes, tired of the question.

"I scanned him this morning," Lia assured her. "No new cellular mutations."

"Good," the psi-hacker nodded. "Now go off and fight evil. Debrief in eight hours."

"Copy that," I replied. "Kato out."

Grace toasted me with her coffee mug and then broke connection.

Six months and she still didn't trust me.

Well, to be fair, Grace once watched me climb through a shadow tunnel and drink a guy's mind. In my defense, the healer (one Archibald Cramm) was using his powers to torture Grace. He was a high-ranking member of The Black Wheel—a group of genocidal one-percenters who wanted to kill the other 99% just to avert a theoretical class war.

Drinking Cramm's mind left him convulsing on the floor with the mentality of a newborn. His life memories were in my head, giving me full access to his past and skill sets. What really freaked Grace out was the part where I jacked the guy's shadow and made it heal her. From day one, Grace insisted I get treated.

Seeing as Grace was sort of a monster herself, I should've listened.

When she was blown up, a rare psychic instability popped up in her head. Left unchecked, it would've turned Grace into a psychic vampire. Luckily, the Outfitter got to her first. The super genius put implants into Grace's head and took her under his wing until he died during *Clean Sweep*. The implants (somehow) contained the instability and stored all of her memories. While Grace could've lived a "normal" life, she didn't see it that way. To her, there would always be a monster in her head.

That's why she was doubly afraid of me.

Me? I liked my short-lived psychic vampire phase. The ability allowed us to tear up The Black Wheel within a matter of weeks (instead of years). Eventually, though, I was getting addicted to the varying flavors of my victims' minds. Then it got to the point where I wondered what Lia's mind tasted like. That's when I sought treatment.

Like any other serious disease, treatments were a pain in the ass.

Just before I died from augmentation failure, Grace had "dosed" me with a nanite package that she modified. The package was codenamed ACHE (Autonomous Command Hierarchical Entity). The portable AI system was designed to keep its host alive and better able to save the world. Funny thing was ACHE didn't save me from death. Nope, I had a shadowporting ninja to thank for that.

A few hours before I died, I ripped his power. Then I shadowported around, jumping from shadow-to-shadow and place-to-place. With each shadowportation, I picked up microbes. Floating within Shadow itself, they were normally harmless in healthy bodies. However, they could infect dead people just fine.

When I died, they began to make me into a full-on shadow beast . . . until ACHE stepped in. The nanites halted the mutation at the 41.83% mark. I awoke with a bunch of new powers and dwindling humanity. Before I asked Grace for help, the nanites were still there—taking up space in my body. To cure me, Grace instructed the AI to reverse the mutation.

Technically, it worked.

I couldn't shadowport across the world anymore. I couldn't regenerate or be full-time strong. Nor could I track people by smell or make shadow objects anymore (I really missed that). Lastly, I couldn't feed on minds. The addiction more or less faded away.

In the end, ACHE made me 82.477% human before Grace was convinced that my mutation was stable. While my powers were watered-the-fuck down, I could eat solid foods again and my blood wasn't black anymore. Eventually, I transferred ACHE to a new host because I was sick of its snobby, asshole personality.

"We need a vehicle," Lia said, returning my thoughts to the present.

"No we don't," I scoffed. "We've got two cars, two SUVs, and a motorcycle in the garage."

"I'm talking something with class," she replied.

"Lemme guess: pink?"

"Fuchsia," Lia said. "With gadgets and stuff."

I didn't even bother mentioning her lack of a license. If I did, Lia would give me a smug grin and then hack the DMV with her laptop. By Friday, she'd present me with a fake ID, insurance, passports, etc. I don't know where she'd get the money to pay for all of that (nor would I want to).

Instead, I took my armored daughter by the hand and headed for the exit tunnel. The titanium doors slid open to reveal a subway-worthy tunnel without rails. It would lead us into the Downtown sewers. From there, we could pop out anywhere in the city and begin our futile crusade for justice.

"Tell ya' what," I joked as I pulled down my mask, "scrape together your allowance money and we'll talk."

"You don't give me an allowance!" Lia melodramatically hissed.

"Hmm," I pretended to contemplate. "Fair enough. How's fifty bucks a week sound?"

I allowed her armored hand to gently smack me in the back of the head.

"Ow!" I winced with mock pain. "Okay, how about eighty bucks?"

Smack!

CHAPTER THREE

Not long into our patrol, we came across Eddie Digonsky, a.k.a., Dr. Wabbit.

The indie pimp had just made the unknowing mistake of gut-punching a whore as we flew past. Wabbit's victim was a waifish hooker in a cheap green mini-skirt, matching heels, and too much makeup. I couldn't tell if her long red hair was real, dyed, or a wig. Barely old enough to drive, the wheezing victim slumped against the side of the alley wall.

That's when Lia signaled me to stop.

Dr. Wabbit turned around as he heard her land behind him. Poor guy. It was bad enough being a white guy with no style. This fucker had everything but the damned pimp hat! Wabbit sported a beige, full-length fur coat draped over his white three-piece suit and matching high tops.

The steroid arms, thinning black hair, and gold braces made me wonder how he got his nickname. Anyone this tacky shouldn't be in the pimp trade—not in this century, anyway. Granted, he managed to keep a decent stable of whores.

Somewhere in his mid-thirties, Wabbit unbuttoned his suit jacket. The fool boldly flashed a gold-plated Desert Eagle .44 that he had tucked in the front his pants.

"Who the fuck are you supposed to be? Joan of Bitch?" he taunted with a cackling laugh.

I didn't bother scanning Wabbit for drugs. Clearly, he was using.

Annoyed, Lia snatched the gun from his pants.

"Hey!" Wabbit shouted.

The pimp tried to muscle his gun from her armored hand. When he couldn't, Wabbit cut loose with an impressive tirade of insults about Lia's sexual orientation. The guy wouldn't shut up until she jammed the gun against his forehead.

"Joan of Bitch," Lia mused. "How's that for a codename?"

Wabbit's eyes went wide as she cocked the hammer. Still in the air, I folded my arms and toyed with it in my head.

"Nah," I replied. "Too Catholic."

"Help a brutha out, man!" Wabbit yelled up at me. "Reign your bitch in!"

He shouldn't have said that.

I tapped my collar, which cut it off. After the two-story drop, I landed with ease on the darkened asphalt. Then I sprang forward and backhanded Wabbit so hard that he went flying. The pimp landed on a pile of garbage bags, half-dazed as I drew my wakizashi. Wabbit's gray eyes widened as my blade glistened under a nearby streetlight.

"You can't kill me, Cly!" he practically shrieked through a bloodied mouth. "The Wungs'll put your ass in a box!"

I stayed my hand and took a few deep breaths.

The four mobs shared the crime in Pillar City. Rather than splitting it into territories, they decided to split the crime itself. The Russians sold weapons—from pepper spray to WMDs. The Colombians handled drugs and black market augmentations. The Irish smuggled whoever/whatever. And the Wung Triad handled sex, gambling, and money laundering. The four mobs stuck to their specialties and actually did business with each other—all to maintain a lucrative peace.

Each mob farmed out some of their enterprises to sub-contractors, like Wabbit. As long as the sub-contractors footed half their profits, they were protected.

Killing this asshole would be like killing a Triad lieutenant. The repercussions wouldn't be survivable.

I slowly sheathed my weapon.

"Is he mobbed up?" Lia asked.

"Afraid so," I replied. "Mess with his earnings and you're dead."

"Technically, I'm dead just for helping you," Lia replied, clearly wanting to empty the clip.

Per the terms of my Community Service, she had a point. I regarded the doe-eyed whore, who eyed us all with a healthy amount of fear.

"What'd she do?" I pointedly asked as Wabbit shakily rose to his feet.

"What she always does!" Wabbit yelled with an angry glance her way. "She came up short!"

"Hmm," I nodded my understanding. "What happens when one of your girls comes up short too often?"

Wabbit gave me an evil grin and looked down at his balls.

"I give 'em a taste of my carrot, then shoot 'em in the face when I've had my fill. Lets the other hos know who's running these blocks."

"How very gangsta'," I rolled my eyes.

The pimp took offense at my remark and narrowed his eyes.

"Get ta' steppin' Cly . . . unless you want the Wungs on you!"

I weighed my options. Then I nodded and backed away a few paces. Certain that I wasn't gonna kill him, the wannabe bent over and picked up his man fur.

"Gimme back my gun," Wabbit told Lia while he brushed bits of garbage from his coat.

As he did, the waifish hooker began to cry like the child she was. Lia walked over, gun in her right hand

and finger on the trigger. Even with armor on, I could tell that she wanted him dead.

If she were someone else's kid, I'd let her end him. Instead, I held out my right hand. Lia wasn't a stone-cold killer. That was my job. If I had anything to say about it, she'd never have to kill ever again. For now, I needed her to play nice. Lia sighed and finally slapped the Desert Eagle into my palm.

"Sorry about my actions, Mr. Wabbit," I said as I ejected the clip, checked the load, and saw that it was full.

"Whatever, dawg," the pimp replied as I reloaded the handgun.

Wabbit slipped the coat back over his shoulders. Trying to regain some lost pride, he expectantly held out his right hand. I took a step toward the pimp . . . and then headed over to the little girl.

"What's your name, sweetheart?" I asked her.

"Juliette," she wept.

I gave her a sympathetic sigh and then handed her the gun. "Give him back his gun, Juliette."

Wabbit's fur fell off him as he turned and ran. Laughingstock that he was, the pimp was fast. Too bad Lia's armor made her faster. The pimp sprinted twenty feet before she caught up to him. Lia grabbed him by the back of his suit collar and easily dragged his sorry ass back to us.

"Go on," I prodded Juliette, "give the man back his gun. Including the bullets."

Juliette was young but she wasn't dumb. She thoughtfully looked down at the hand cannon.

"What the fuck you doin'?!" Wabbit yelled as Lia towered over him. "That's my bitch! Mine!"

"Well, Juliette," I sighed to the girl, "if you 'give' him every bullet in that clip, he won't leave you dead in a dumpster, right?"

Trembling, Juliette looked over at her pimp. The girl had been on these streets long enough to know that mercy wasn't an option. At best, Wabbit would put her in the hospital. More than likely, she'd end up in a dumpster with two bullets in the face. Her case would be deemed "unsolved" by the cops, who were paid good money not to care.

"Your choice," I said as I walked away.

Lia shoved Wabbit toward the girl. The pimp was ten feet away from his frightened employee. He glared at Lia and then eyed Juliette.

"C'mon, Julie! I was just playin', girl," Wabbit grinned, clearly full of shit, "I'd never hurt you."

The pimp stopped in his tracks when Juliette raised the massive gun in a two-handed grip. Tiny finger on the trigger. Barrel aimed at his balls. I pulled my mask up. It self-configured to that of a pirate head scarf, allowing the sweet smell of garbage to offend my nose. I pulled out the Marlboros.

"Maybe you should buy her flowers," I muttered as I fished out a cigarette with my teeth. "Chicks love flowers."

Wabbit ignored me and kept his eyes on the gun.

"Give me the gun, baby," he said with a fake smile. "C'mon. Give me the gun."

The girl trembled as the pimp inched a bit closer . . .

"Gimme the gun, bitch!" Wabbit yelled as he rushed her from seven feet away.

In retrospect, I think he was expecting her to freeze; that she'd be too chickenshit to kill *the* Dr. Wabbit. Instead, Juliette looked away and blasted him once, twice, and then some. She kept pulling the trigger long after the clip was empty. Most of her shots punched through his chest and hit the brick wall on the other side of the alley.

Sprawled out on the alleyway, Wabbit's lifeless eyes stared upward.

"That was fun," I said as I walked past Lia and headed toward the mouth of the alley.

"You think we'll get in trouble?" Lia nervously asked after we walked a few blocks.

She was right to be afraid. Yeah, we had super powers and nice toys. Then again, so did the Wungs. The Triad was a global operation with thousands of gun-toting street soldiers at their disposal. If they wanted us dead, we'd end up that way. The pedestrians cleared a path for us, intrigued by Lia's armor and flat-out scared of me. Halfway through my cigarette, I glanced over at her.

"Even if the Wungs bothered to look for his killer, they wouldn't mind his death."

"Why's that?" she asked. "Because 'Wabbit's' a stupid name for a pimp?"

"That's one reason," I smiled. "The other is that they can sell his turf to someone else for a higher price. After all, Wabbit did build up his little franchise."

"You think she'll make it off the streets?" she asked.

"Juliette?" I paused. "No."

Lia shook her head.

"I should've left it alone, huh?"

I shrugged. "Since you didn't, that means you're a better person than me. Just don't let your scruples get you killed."

Lia stared at me. I knew what she was thinking on the other side of that armored mask. Just as I was about to suggest we resume our patrol, she turned around and started back toward the alley.

"What are you doing?" I asked without turning around, a proud smile on my face.

"Saving the girl," Lia replied before leaping into the air.

There were "oooh's" and "aaah's" as she flew back to the alley. Seeing as super heroes were a rare sight in this town, I guess they had good reason. I tapped the cigarette against my mouthpiece radio. Then I kept on walking.

"Lia, get her out of town," I advised.

"Where to?" came her reply. "Canada?"

"I don't wanna know. Bug Grace and follow her advice. She knows how to hide someone."

"Will do," Lia replied. "Sorry about the mess, Dad."

"Don't be," I sighed. "The world's better without that dickhead. Besides, you're in charge tonight, remember?"

"Call you when I get back," she replied. "Be safe."

I broke contact with a slight chuckle. Safe was a forgotten part of my vocabulary. I finished my cigarette and tossed it into a sewer. Then I pulled my mask down and turned around. A few seconds later, I saw Lia flying away with Juliette in her arms. I'd have to toss the Wungs some serious bribe money to make this go away. Otherwise, they'd lose face—

My thoughts were interrupted by the sounds of screeching tires and oncoming police sirens. A white, late-model Charger roared around a corner with four police cars in pursuit. They were headed my way. This looked fun.

I drew my wakizashi and leaped at the fleeing vehicle. Covered up by the costume, my darkness-enhanced strength was holding up just fine. The driver didn't bother to swerve, allowing me to leap high and then land on the hood. I grabbed the upper edge of it with my right hand. The blade was in my left as I looked inside and sized up the three guys inside.

According to the goggles, the one in the front passenger seat was dead . . . and familiar. It was Nolan Fricks, which was sadly ironic because he was one of the best wheelmen I've ever seen. He had the sophistication of a rural farm hand, but when it came to fast cars he was a god. Nolan worked freelance, driving for shit money. He'd take on any well-planned job that came with a suitable risk. The adrenaline rush was all he was after.

As a fixer, I hired him from time-to-time. I even tried to recruit him. Too bad Nolan wouldn't commit to anything but the next job. That's how he rolled. Blond-haired and average looking, he was buckled into the seat with a triple-tap chest wound. His beige shirt and black denim jeans were splattered with his blood. Somewhere in his late 30's, his skin hadn't gone pale yet.

What a waste.

In the driver's seat was Kevin Freemont, a.k.a. Glue. In his early 40's, the lean black mastermind had an impressive track record for results. The pair had worked together in the past. Being a professional kidnapper, Glue valued someone with Nolan's skill.

Glue specialized in complex abductions, rather than mere snatch-and-grabs. I think he preferred the challenge. When I heard of him, some four years back, I almost approached him. I ended changing my mind though.

The guy was an over-hyped crook; the type of who didn't bother trying to be the best in his field. Glue simply did two or three jobs a year, and then fucked around until he was broke enough to want the next one. To me, that mentality made him a part-time, disposable talent. Someone who lacked the balls to do the heavy shit jobs that my mercs used to manage.

It was clear (from the initial shock and fear) that Glue recognized me. Dressed in black, he wore a harness full of toys that a cat burglar might use, including a SIG Sauer in a left shoulder holster. He gripped the wheel with his left hand. His right went for the pistol.

Because of their back-seat passenger, I didn't kill Glue outright. Instead, I stabbed the wakizashi through the windshield, stopping a few inches shy of his heart. Then I mouthed the words "pull over." Glue eyed my blade and then shook his head as he made a wild left turn. Curious, I looked over my left shoulder and realized that he was heading for St. George's Hospital.

Maybe he thought Nolan was still alive.

I glanced up at the sounds of incoming gunfire from the pursuing cops. Bullets pinged off the Charger and left holes through the windows. Judging from the way bullets were bouncing off my armored cloth, the cops were more interested in killing me than arresting Glue. Rumor was that any cop who brought me down would have his/her career fast-tracked, courtesy of Police Commissioner Harris. Annoyed, I sheathed my blade and regarded the six cop cars on our tail. They should've known better than to bust caps with so many bystanders in the area.

That's greed for ya.

I reached for a brown slicker grenade and flicked it over the roof of the car. The pill-sized device landed behind us and then exploded. A fast-spreading gas emerged, which liquefied in a half-second over an impossibly wide area. The effect was akin to an oil slick, only the stuff was clear as water. Each of the pursuing cop cars rolled through it, spun out of control, and then slammed into parked cars and/or each other.

Glue gawked up at me through the windshield. Guess he was wondering why I had helped him. With my free hand, I knocked on the bullet-riddled windshield, pointed at Nolan, and then ran my fingertips back-and-forth across my neck. Never taking his eyes off me, the kidnapper holstered his gun. With both hands on the wheel, Glue raced around an ambulance and then skidded to a stop in front of the ER.

Glue then reached over and quickly checked Nolan's pulse. I hopped off the hood as he punched the dashboard with frustration.

"Friend of yours?" I asked.

"Fuck off, Cly!" the kidnapper scowled as he opened the door and climbed out.

Short and wiry, Glue got out of the driver's seat and stormed off. I watched him leave, and then swapped glances with his equally confused hostage. The boy (no older than twelve) was strapped in with a seat belt. His hands were flex cuffed behind him. Someone had stuck a black-and-purple ball gag in his mouth, as well as an inhibitor collar around his neck. The crimson device turned off the powers of any (well, most) supers who wore them.

I wondered about the kid's powers.

The boy mumbled through the gag, probably something to the effect of "Get me the fuck out of here!" Dressed in beige slacks, a navy-blue blazer, white shirt, and red tie, the kid probably came from a rich home. Rich kids annoyed me. The richer the parents, the more obnoxious their offspring tended to become. Any kid with a ball gag in his mouth had to be a heavyweight champion snob.

"Forgetting your hostage?" I shouted.

Glue ignored me. Instead, he walked across the parking lot, stopping next to a parked blue Durango. He pulled something out of his harness and began to break into the vehicle. The kidnapper popped the lock and started the SUV inside of fifty seconds. He then backed it out and rolled toward the Charger.

The kidnapper put the stolen Durango in park and then got out. Instead of going for the kid, he popped the trunk. I walked around to join him. Inside were two large gray bags. He grabbed one and slung it over his back.

"The other one was Nolan's share," Glue said to me. "Keep it."

Curious, I unzipped the bag. Inside were stacks of money in used, large-denomination notes. Based on the weight, I was guessing . . . five million. This didn't make any goddamned sense. Glue ransomed a hostage for ten million and then kept the hostage? It wasn't his style—unless the exchange went south.

The kidnapper opened the Durango's back door and threw his bag inside. He closed the door as a nervous security guard stepped out, hand on his holstered gun. The fat, balding guard looked to be in his post-cop sixties. He eyed the hostage, the corpse, and then my mask. The guard tried to draw his gun. Only, it wouldn't leave the holster. The guard cursed as he tried to pull it out with both hands, only to realize that they were stuck to the butt of his gun.

"What the hell?!" the guard barked with a thick Jersey accent.

That's why they called him Glue.

He only had one power, an adhesion field, which he rarely used. I don't remember the particulars of said ability—only that it allowed him to make things stick together with tons of force. Most super criminals loved integrating their powers into their heists. Glue, on the other hand, relied on sound planning, years of experience, and qualified accomplices. He only used his power for moments like this one.

Glue calmly walked over to the guard with a spray tube in his left hand. The old man saw it coming but couldn't do shit (not with his feet rooted to the asphalt). The crook sprayed the guard in the face, and then turned away as the old man dropped. The unconscious guard snored as Glue slipped past me. Okay, this guy still wasn't good enough to work for me . . . but he had style.

"What about the kid?" I asked.

Glue stopped for a moment and then scowled at the hostage. Still screaming through his gag, the kid didn't want to shut up.

"Free advice?" Glue asked. "Shoot his ass. Then hide on another continent."

"Why?" I asked. "Who is he?"

Glue slipped the tube of knockout spray back into his harness.

"Malcolm O'Flernan."

CHAPTER FOUR

"Who the fuck is Malcolm O'Flernan?" I blinked.

"Connor's kid," Glue impatiently replied.

Connor O'Flernan was Seamus' youngest boy. He and his brother Angus died in a car bombing over a decade ago. Only thing was I didn't know Connor had a fuckin' kid. In theory, Malcolm O'Flernan was an heir to the O'Flernan empire—especially if Seamus wrote a secret will just for his grandson.

Glue turned to leave. I plucked a transparent tracking disc from my utility sash and slipped it under the second bag.

"Wait," I said, "you're gonna need all the cash you can get."

The rationale made Glue pause with his back to me. I pulled the second bag out of the Charger's trunk. The sizeable load was light to me as I walked over to the back door, opened it, and then tossed the bag of cash inside. Glue warily looked on with his hand near the SIG.

"You're letting me go?"

"Why not?" I shrugged. "You're about to be marked for death by the O'Flernan mob. Knowing what that's like, you get a pass."

Glue nodded as he lowered his gun hand. Guess he knew about my unique "arrangement" with the mobs.

"I didn't know Connor had a kid," I admitted.

"That was the old man's intention," Glue replied. "He kept the little shit off the grid."

"Then why'd you kidnap him?" I frowned. "Isn't that suicide?"

"Not if Seamus O'Flernan hired me to do it," Glue replied as he headed for the driver's seat. "I'm outta here."

"Wait!" I followed him. "Seamus hired you to kidnap his own grandson?!'"

Glue stopped with the driver's side door half-closed.

"Three years ago, Seamus put me on retainer for one job, worth $200 million."

I gave a low whistle at the ridiculous sum. Glue should've walked away from the gig (and maybe he tried). Too bad Seamus O'Flernan didn't take "no" from anyone. In fact, that's why I had him killed last year.

"I was supposed to snatch the grandkid within six months of Seamus' death," Glue continued.

"Then what?"

"Deliver him to Harlan Ronns," Glue replied. "It took me months to assemble a team, find the kid, and then figure a way past the security."

This didn't make sense.

Seamus would've stashed the kid somewhere far from here and with plenty of O'Flernan protection. So why not just have them deliver the kid to Ronns when he died? Why would Glue have to "find" the boy at all? The old man must've had his reasons. Stranger still, Seamus didn't put me on retainer to grab the kid. As a fixer, I would've seen the caper done right.

Instead, he relied on a second-stringer who lacked the proper resources. It was almost like he wanted Glue to fail . . .

"What went wrong?" I asked.

"Everything," Glue replied as he lowered the power windows and slammed the door. "Seamus left an extra $10 million in an account to cover expenses. The second I touched it, we got hounded. Multiple kill teams targeted us. Two of my guys were killed. Two more bailed. By the time Nolan and I found the kid, I had to break into a fortified compound and get him out on my own!"

"Why didn't you just take the money and vanish?" I asked.

"I'm a professional, Cly," Glue replied with a hint of annoyance. "That means I see my jobs through to the end."

Without another word, the kidnapper hit the gas and sped away.

I watched the Durango disappear into the night, thinking that (maybe) Glue wasn't second-rate after all. Then I walked over to the Charger. Nurses and patients were gathering around the snoring guard. I should stay out of this because this kid's fate was sealed in a bad way. If I left him there, he'd be killed by his own fucking mob.

Deidre O'Flernan—his aunt—would happily see to it.

Once a spoiled little party girl, she was Seamus' only surviving child. The old man hadn't groomed her to run his mob. He wanted her to remain an outsider, marry a decent Irish Catholic, and give him grandsons. Instead, Deidre lived a rebellious life of debauchery. At twenty-eight, it didn't look like she'd ever outgrow her booze-and-drugs lifestyle.

As fate would have it, I was the one who ruined her fun.

Within an hour of Seamus' death, I met with representatives of the four mobs, including Harlan Ronns. Ronns was an O'Flernan Shepherd (a fancy way of saying "regional chief enforcer"). During that meeting, I showed them a recording of Seamus O'Flernan trying to fuck me over. After his three bodyguards tried to kill me, I had him executed. At the time, I didn't know that Seamus' protection detail were undercover FBI agents. That would've been reason enough to cap the old man.

No, his execution was cold, hard math. Seamus was so dangerous an enemy that he had to die right then and there. Had I let him live, he'd have done whatever else it took to make me do his bidding–like kidnapping Lia. My peace of mind was the real reason Seamus O'Flernan had to die.

Trying to salvage the situation (and avert any unnecessary power vacuums), I suggested that Ronns have Deidre "kidnapped" and psi-trained. The kidnapping would raise public sympathy. The psi-training would turn her into a suitable mob boss overnight.

Even though Ronns swore that he'd kill me, the fucker actually took my advice. They grabbed Deidre off some tropical resort and stuck her in a room with Seamus' top underbosses. The psi-training was essentially a transfusion of knowledge—from them to her. Within a few hours, Deidre O'Flernan went from college dropout to seasoned mob boss.

Her first course of action was to fire Harlan Ronns. As far as Deidre was concerned, Ronns was responsible for Seamus' safety and should've died protecting him that night. Instead, he was on a Wung pleasure ship (*The Depravity*) getting his dick wet. Last I heard, the ex-Shepherd packed up his family and left town in disgrace.

Deidre then proceeded to consolidate her grip on the family operations. Some of the more arrogant underbosses refused to answer to the former party slut. They tried to strike out on their own . . . and she made an example of them. Their efficiently brutal deaths made the remaining underbosses fall in line. Then she started taking over smaller (independent) smuggling operations and a slew of new clients. These days, the O'Flernan mob was stronger than ever.

That's why young Malcolm had to die.

The last thing Deidre would want was for a prep school thumbsucker to come out of nowhere and claim her mob throne. If I were still a fixer, I'd advise her to put young Malcolm in the ground. Love her or hate her, Deidre was the more logical choice to run things.

As a crime fighter, that wasn't an option. I turned toward the little shit and gave him an evil smile. I had a chance to kick the Irish bastards where it hurt, while conforming to the demands of my Community Service. Guess that was reason enough to be the good guy tonight.

A plump little nurse was heading toward the Charger. She found Malcolm and started to unfasten his seat belt. I walked over and shoved her away. Her eyes widened at the sight of me. As she ran off, I leaned in and sized up the little menace. He looked back at me with a surprising defiance in his black eyes, like he expected me to end him right then and there.

Once folks started putting bounties on Malcolm's head, the boy might wish I had.

Malcolm O'Flernan hungrily put down two steak dogs, a side of fries, and a Cherry Coke. I sat next to him with the ball gag in a coat pocket. The inhibitor collar was still around his neck, only because I didn't have the special key to unlock it. I could've sliced it off but the device might've been rigged to blow. When I explained this to Malcolm, he grudgingly agreed it was best to leave it on.

Once I flew him here and took my mask off, the kid actually relaxed. Maybe he (somehow) knew my face and my rep for not killing children. Although it was almost ten at night, I figured Malcolm needed more food than sleep. As he ate, I sipped my malt and enjoyed a smoke. This stretch of 49th Street was in Downtown's business district. Right now, it was practically deserted. Nestled amidst the jungle of old buildings was *Smitty's Dog Shack*.

Barely half the size of a typical McDonald's restaurant, the white-painted building was over eighty years old. The narrow, rectangular hot dog stand had six metal stools set in front for customers to sit while they ate. The red-cushioned stools were ripped out of the sidewalk about once every decade. Open 24/7, the hot dog stand survived mainly by being the best place to eat within ten blocks—gourmet or otherwise. Other eateries came and went in this cutthroat part of town but *Smitty's* outlasted them all.

Its current owner, Charlie Metts, was a former drug smuggler who served eighteen years. He learned to cook in prison. When Metts got out, he (literally) dug up some of his old wealth and bought the place. The previous owner, Barney Clime, used to fence stolen property out of here until colon cancer ended him. With a staff of three cooks to back him up, Metts planned to work the grill until his dying day. In his early forties, the large man had grayish stubble and mahogany skin. Oddly enough, he ran an honest joint even though it would've been the perfect criminal front.

Guess he was afraid of going back inside.

Tonight, Metts wore the standard uniform of comfortable black shoes, black cotton slacks, a white button-down shirt, and a black-and-white apron with *Smitty's* stenciled across the front. Metts let his people wear whatever caps or hairnets they saw fit. He favored the round, cotton caps that some surgeons wore when they worked.

Ray Charles' *Unchain My Heart* played in the background as Metts hastily scribbled down a list of supplies he'd have to order for next week. A righty, his huge hand wielded the cheap blue pen with a crisp cursive.

"Care for a refill?" Metts nodded my way.

"Sure," I replied before I leaned in and polished off my chocolate-and-vodka malt. The drink did wonders for my mood. While this place didn't have a liquor license, we were in Pillar City (where no one gave a fuck).

Metts took my large cup and stepped away.

"You full?" I asked the kid.

Malcolm nodded. "Thanks for taking that gag out of my mouth."

"Seemed a bit like overkill for a quiet kid like you," I replied through a mouthful of smoke. "So, what now?"

Malcolm sized me up for a moment.

"I want to get the hell out of here," he admitted, "but there's family business to sort out."

"Your grandfather's last will and testament?" I asked.

"Something like that," Malcolm replied with a weird smile. "I'm sorry you had to kill him."

So, the young heir was up on current events.

"I hope you don't carry grudges," I told him.

"Sometimes," Malcolm replied, before he sipped his drink. "But I don't have any beefs with you, Mr. Cly. I just want to settle my family's estate."

"As far as your aunt's concerned, it *is* settled," I replied. "You do know that Deidre will have you killed, right? Even if Seamus left a signed will for you to find."

"She'll try," Malcolm replied without concern.

"You mean to take over the mob by force?"

Malcolm shook his head. "I actually want to make it legit."

"Why?" I grinned. "Damned thing's worth billions as it is."

"So would a legitimate shipping empire," argued the naïve kid.

Young Malcolm apparently didn't understand the true nature of the O'Flernan mob. These fuckers supplied fast, protected, and discreet shipping with no questions asked. That "service" earned them friends in every corner of the world. They were on a first-name basis with most of the powerful individuals on this planet (from politicians to organized crime bosses to genocidal lunatics). Their very satisfied customers often did them favors as a result.

Even if Malcolm killed Deidre and took over the mob, the underbosses would outright rebel against him and the notion of honest business. Going legit would cost them billions, not to mention their contacts and protected influence. Worse, their lesser rivals would surge in, eager to steal the O'Flernans' grip on the global smuggling market. My guess was that their mob would be on the ropes within a year.

Maybe that's why I was smiling.

Metts came back with my malt and then paused. He looked passed my shoulder with evident concern on his face.

"What?" I asked, taking my malt from his hand.

"Two really big guys are heading over here," Metts said. "I don't think they're here for the food."

"Thanks," I sighed as I handed the malt back and pulled my mask down.

Blocked from the light, my body's super strength instantly returned just as I casually turned around. The two white guys briskly walked toward us, both in black suits, overcoats, and fedoras. Big and intimidating, they looked like the type of goons you sent to break bones and/or fetch people. My guess? They were O'Flernan.

"May I help you, gentlemen?" I asked through my mask.

"Give us the kid, Cly," said the guy on the left.

I admired his well-trimmed mustache for a moment and then shook my head.

"You two look like trouble," I mused aloud. "Besides, this young fellow's my guest. I'll be showing him the town while he's here."

"Last chance," said the clean-shaven guy on the right. "Then I get to smear your ass all over this street."

I raised a scolding right index finger and wagged it at him.

"You can't fight me," I countered. "Doing so is a violation of the Community Service deal. If I don't kill you, your boss will."

The two men shared grins, indicating that they knew something I didn't. Maybe their powers were making them cocky. Without my power gaze, I couldn't tell what they could do. Frankly, I'd be offended if Deidre had sent normal humans to take the kid from me, so I'd have to assume the worst. Speaking of which, how'd she find Malcolm so fast?

"Um . . . Mr. Cly," Malcolm pointed behind me.

I sighed as I felt the barrel of Metts' 12-gauge pressed against the back of my head.

"You weren't supposed to take them here!" Metts hissed.

"Orders are orders," said the guy on the left.

"*Et tu*, Metts?" I teased.

"Hand your guns over, Cly," Metts ordered.

I carefully drew my Glocks and handed them to the guy on the right, who snatched them up and pointed them at me. The one on the left slugged me in the stomach. My costume sucked up the impact. I sagged forward with a fake groan and then slowly sat up again. The mustached mobster glanced over at his pal and chuckled.

"All that muscle and he can't take a punch —"

The fucker might've said more had I not reached back and grabbed Mett's shotgun by the barrel. By the time the big man's finger pulled the trigger, I had shoved it toward the guy with my guns. Malcolm winced at the blast . . . and then frowned with surprise.

To be honest, so did I.

The buckshot floated in the air, less than an inch from the mobster's face. My goggles alerted me to a magnetic field. Fuck! The goon on the left was a magslinger—the street slang assigned to supers with the ability to move metal via magnetic fields. That level of precision implied that he was damned good with his power.

"Kill 'em," spat the magslinger as he let the buckshot fall to the sidewalk.

His partner grinned as he cut loose with my guns. Metts took a few hits to the head and chest. As his corpse fell behind the counter, I hopped in front of Malcolm and shielded him. My costume made the bullets feel like hard-thrown peanuts instead of .45-caliber rounds. Over the ringing gunshots I could hear Metts' staff scream as they ran toward the rear exit.

The second the clips went dry, the shooter's cocky smile dropped as I turned and rushed him. The fucker released a purplish gas as I grabbed his throat with my left hand. Like a whole-body fart, the gas just came out from under his suit in all directions.

I glanced over at the magslinger, who looked on with amusement as he backed away from the gas cloud. My mask's filter protected me but Malcolm wasn't so lucky. I turned toward the kid as I heard his coughs. Instead of dropping, the kid's eyes went vacant and his stance went utterly docile. The gaseous super dropped my Glocks and tried to pry my hand free with both of his . . . and failed.

The goggles flashed a warning about the presence of mind control gas. Relieved that it wasn't some kind of acid or nerve agent, I lifted the fucker into air and slowly crushed his throat.

"You can let me go now," wheezed the red-faced super.

I guess he didn't know about my filter.

"Just a sec," I replied as I crushed his windpipe. The gas guy's eyes went lifeless as I lobbed him at his pal.

The magslinger angrily sidestepped the flying body while I rushed in to kill him next. The super narrowed his eyes. Just before I could grab him, his field lifted me off the sidewalk. With all the metal on me, I shouldn't have been too surprised. The magslinger smirked before he sent me flying across the street. A parking meter broke my fall. If not for the costume, he'd have snapped my spine.

I rolled onto my stomach and tried to rise . . . but couldn't. Odds were that he was pinning me to the curb with my utility harness. While I struggled, the magslinger picked up a Ford Focus, floated it over (upside-down), and then dropped it on me.

"I'll be with you in a second, Cly," the magslinger shouted with a taunting smile.

Pinned under the car, I looked over and saw the magslinger turn toward Malcolm. The fucker pulled out a Glock of his own and casually racked the slide.

Six months ago, I could've easily flipped the car off or killed this guy with shadow weapons. Now, the best I could do was to assume a push-up position with about a ton of car on my aching back. At least the fucker didn't feed the car with a residual charge. If he had, I'd be stuck to the Focus like a fridge magnet. Luckily, there were streetlights around. They gave off enough shadows for me to try a shadowport.

Shadowportation, as a power, was something of a mystery among experts. One-part psychics and nine-parts dimensional travel, it allowed a wielder to move from one shadow to another. I could picture a target and then create a shadow tunnel to get there from anywhere in the world. Since my mutation therapy, my power's range had fallen to about 80 yards.

It would have to do.

The O'Flernan goon cocked the hammer and aimed for the boy's vacant face. I scrambled into the Ford's shadow. The swirling black energy of the shadow tunnel whizzed past for a second. I drew the Colt with my left hand, half-spun, and then fell out of the shadow of *Smitty's* front awning. The magslinger fired a split-second before I did.

His bullet harmlessly flattened against my right shoulder, just as I dropped in front of Malcolm. My non-ferrous Embedder round caught him in the sternum. The magslinger's eyes widened in shock and pain as he fell into his own shadow—which I turned into a tunnel at the last instant.

Destination: inside of the solid-looking building across the street.

Malcolm still stood there like a living mannequin. I grabbed the kid and managed to toss him over the counter before the Embedder round exploded. The force of the blast surged across the street and bounced me off the counter. I hit the sidewalk and covered my head as bits of building rained past me. Then I looked up at the burning structure, which was missing about two floors' worth of its façade.

The gas super's phone began to ring.

With a groan, I retrieved it from his pocket. The caller ID read *Boss Lady*, which could only mean Deidre O'Flernan. Fuck it. I didn't want to go to war with the Irish but I wasn't stupid enough to think it wouldn't happen someday. All the bitch needed was an excuse . . . which I had just given her.

I let the phone go to voicemail as I stood up and eyed the destruction. Then I got the weirdest idea. As car and fire alarms blared all around me, I turned my back to the carnage and lifted up my mask. Then I cracked a smile as I took a fuckin' selfie with the dead guy's phone. Pleased by the pic, I e-mailed a copy to Grace, stomped the phone to pieces, and then flew Malcolm the fuck out of there.

CHAPTER FIVE

"What the hell have you done?!" Grace snapped through my radio.

"If you want me to give him to the Irish, just ask me nicely," I replied. "Right now, tell Lia to stay out of the city."

I paced the rooftop of the Patterson Building with Malcolm slung over my right shoulder. The convenient old skyscraper was about four blocks away from *Smitty's* and offered me a wonderful vantage point. The firefighters and paramedics started showing up a few minutes ago, simply because they gave more of a shit than the cops did.

"What about you?" Grace pressed. "You need to leave the country and take him with you!"

"I don't run," I sighed. "Now shut up and give me a safe location to crash."

"Anything specific?" she asked.

"I need a healer and some trustworthy idiots willing to babysit our guy here."

There was a pause.

"Hold," Grace growled.

Physically, I felt the hints of the various aches and pains that tomorrow would bring. Superhuman or not, I wasn't getting any younger. I set Malcolm on his feet and gave him a quick med scan. The kid had a facial bruise (from when I threw him). And, for some reason, his black eyes were now blue. Other than that, he was simply zombified.

Maybe the eye color thing was a side effect of the gas. Guess I should've asked that mob fucker before I killed him. Hopefully, it would wear off in a few hours. 'Til then, my job was to keep young Malcolm from earning a slot in the morgue.

"Head for Uptown," Grace said. "Gratte's got a team at 401 Jove Street. They've agreed to keep an eye on your friend."

"Tell them that they've gotta remove a Mark-10 inhibitor collar," I added. "I'll pay for the labor."

"No need," she replied. "I've already wired them more than enough money."

"Thanks, Grace," I muttered as I tapped my flight collar. "Needless to say, I'll need digital overwatch for the next few days."

"Like it'll save you," she half-joked.

"Here's to hoping," I replied. "By the by, make yourself harder to find."

"I hope you know what you're doing," Grace replied before breaking contact.

I picked up the kid and took to the air.

The collar headed for Underpass 2, one of four highways connecting Uptown and Downtown. Shaped like a giant corkscrew, the six-lane structure had a hollow core and plenty of traffic. I flew up into it with my mind racing.

I had to assume that Deidre O'Flernan was more ruthless than her father. Once she knew of my involvement, she'd hit me where I was weak. That meant that my few remaining contacts could end up getting snatched and/or killed. I was mainly worried about Lia and Juanita.

As a fixer, my typical reaction to making a new enemy would be to kill that enemy. The problem here was that I didn't have my firm (and its small army) anymore. Even if I could kill Deidre O'Flernan tonight, I wouldn't survive the guaranteed O'Flernan retribution. They had enough money, connections, and numbers to topple a small country. The direct approach wouldn't work.

No. I'd have to fight dirty.

*　*　*

I arrived at 401 Jove Street to find what used to be the *Jensky & Sons Furniture Warehouse*. Out-of-business for years, the massive, brick building was surrounded by a large asphalt parking area. Knowing Gratte, a site this large would end up converted into a variable-use stash house.

In a place like Pillar City, all types of cargo needed to be tucked out of sight: whether it was a stolen art collection or a bunch of illegals destined for some nearby sweatshop. Many of Pillar City's high-end stash houses were put together by a company called *Lairs 'R Us.*

In business since 2004, D'Angelo "Leo" Gratte ran the enterprise as a two-sided coin. Legally, they designed custom lairs for eccentric types with too much money. Pay 'em enough and they could, for example, turn your basement into a quality replica of a medieval wizard's lab, the bridge of a Klingon warbird, or Sherlock Holmes' private study.

They were famous, respected, and made a tidy profit doing what they did.

Their lesser-known (and very illegal) activities involved building lairs, vaults, and/or stash houses of the genuine kind. Gratte had done work for terrorists, government agencies, and everyone in between. All four of the local mobs swore by them. The price-to-quality ratio of *Lairs 'R Us* just couldn't be matched. Also, Gratte's people threw in any desired extras: torture rooms, safe rooms, booby traps, arsenal space, and so on.

The coolest thing of all was that I still owned them.

Lairs 'R Us was my idea—a way to make some quick money and gain valuable intel at the same time. I hired Gratte to be my front man. He kept seventy percent of the profits, while the rest discreetly went to me. His people would slip passive bugs into everything they ever built (even the legit projects). Most of our devices were never found. The few that were never got traced back to us.

Gratte would keep tabs on whatever went down and alerted me whenever something warranted my attention. The inside info had proven priceless over the years. His rep as a freelancer meant that everyone—even my enemies—went to him for jobs, allowing me to spy on them . . . even now.

Unfortunately, when the mobs took my cash, they also went for my properties. It was a good thing that the only ties they found between my firm and *Lairs 'R Us* were fake receipts. Had the bosses learned that Gratte and his people were mine, they'd have killed us all. To date, only Gratte, Lia, and Grace knew about this little arrangement.

I arrived to find three gray *Lairs 'R Us* vans in the back parking lot. Before landing, I scanned the area. Aside from Gratte's well-hidden motion sensors, the lot was clean. I carried Malcolm toward the back door of the two-story structure. Diglet opened the thick metal door and waved me in. The redneck super had a short, thin frame that looked deceptively weak. His gray *Lairs 'R Us* uniform was covered with dust and splotches of mayo. His matching work cap was on backwards.

"Hey Diglet," I greeted him with a relieved smile.

"What's goin' on, Cly?" Diglet replied with his nasally, rapid-fire tone.

It was easy to underestimate the twentysomething craftsman. Pasty-faced and nerdy, he looked like a grease monkey with self-esteem issues. In reality, Diglet was so jittery because he was a tunneler (hence the nickname).

Sadly, this sub-type of natural-born speedster couldn't run fast. Their speed only seemed to work from the waist-up. Diglet, for example, could drop to all fours and tunnel his way through a paved road in under a minute. Granted, this ability wouldn't get the guy his own comic book. Still, such an ability saved Gratte a fortune in terms of equipment and work time.

"Is Band-Aid here?" I asked as Diglet let me pass.

"Yeah," he replied with a curious look at Malcolm. "Back here."

We stood in a narrow hallway. Old and musty, it was lined with about a dozen battery-powered lanterns. I followed Diglet into the back showroom. The large space had six different holes tunneled through its concrete floor. I imagine each one led (or will lead) into a sub-level room of some kind.

Mounds of dirt were everywhere, each twenty feet high. Speck walked up to one with a dustpan. In her late forties, the curly brunette gave me a curt nod before she touched the massive mound and shrank it to mere inches. She then pulled a whiskbroom from her coverall's left pocket and casually swept it into the dustpan.

The shrinkage effect was permanent, unless she undid her own work. Speck could shrink tons of machinery to the size of Tonka toys or smaller. Her power worked on living and non-living matter. Like most shrinkers, she had to make physical contact with the target for her power to kick in.

Even in dirty coveralls, the super looked classy enough to have been someone's executive secretary. Yet, my goggles picked up three guns concealed within her uniform. I always figured Speck to have been retired black ops. It stood to reason that she'd work with Gratte, whose construction gigs tended to be (mostly) safe, well-paying, and allowed for travel.

When I tried to pull up Speck's background, my best people came up blank, which impressed me. Intrigued, I tried to recruit her (on a probationary basis) back in '07. She politely declined, satisfied with her current duties. However, Speck did do the occasional bit of freelance work (usually during tax season).

"What's this place gonna be?" I asked, looking around the newly installed wiring.

"Beats me," Diglet lied with a friendly shrug.

He didn't know that I was his real boss. What he did know was that Gratte didn't want him discussing company biz with outsiders. I approved.

Diglet led me toward the second hole on the left. As we passed the others, I could see Gratte's regular guys. Most of them were ex-cons and/or homeless guys he picked up off the street. All of them were human, hard-working bastards with decent psi-training—both in terms of building skills and work ethics. For a grouchy womanizer, Leo Gratte had a weak spot for losers.

We peered down to find Band-Aid. The cute, round-faced super sat cross-legged on a purple blanket. Eyes closed, she had assumed a meditative posture. The chocolate-skinned healer was wearing dyed-blonde cornrows under her cap. Her coveralls were clean because she knew diddlyshit about construction. Band-Aid's job was two-fold. She healed anyone who needed healing. Second, she was in charge of overwatch.

The only thing all healers had in common was that they could heal people–usually via touch. Everything else was up in the air because natural-born healers (depending on their lineage) typically had other powers too. Band-Aid, for example, could track the life signs and physical health of anyone within a quarter-mile radius.

If someone got so much as a paper cut, she'd sense it. Then, without moving a muscle, she'd psychically reach out into that person's mind, tap into the body's ability to heal, and then deal with the injury. Band-Aid's power was also good for dealing with fatigue. With her power and Gratte's psi-training, his regular guys could work 24 hours straight without really minding it.

Of course, if someone decided to trespass, Band-Aid could do evil wonders as well. While working in Japan last year, a few Yakuza guys tried to extort money from the site foreman. She locked onto all twelve crooks and indefinitely paralyzed them before they made it beyond the perimeter.

Another time, a saboteur had slipped onto one of her project sites with a firebomb. Band-Aid gave the would-be bomber a severe stroke and then had one of Gratte's guys disarm the weapon. Based on the lairs they've built, bomb disposal was a necessary part of the skill package.

"Hey Band-Aid," I smiled. "Could you look this kid over?"

"He'll be fine in a few hours," she replied. "I could wake him up now or let him get some sleep."

"Let him sleep," I replied, relieved that the effect wasn't permanent.

Eyes still closed, the healer turned her head toward me . . . and frowned.

"You, on the other hand, are fucked."

Her words bothered me as I gently laid Malcolm down on his back.

"What do you mean?" I asked.

"I mean that you've been poisoned," Band-Aid replied, "on a genetic level."

"When?" I asked, wondering if Metts had slipped something into my vodka malt.

Band-Aid bobbed her head left-to-right, clearly about to make an educated guess.

"I'm thinking about . . . two months ago. Your organs are suffused with this shit."

I looked down at my torso and tapped my goggles.

"Full medscan," I ordered.

The goggles hummed for a soft moment, then gave me a NEGATIVE reading.

"My sensors say I'm fine," I frowned her way. "You sure about this?"

Band-Aid gave me a "don't-be-stupid" frown.

"I feel fine —" I started to argue.

"Only you're not," Band-Aid interrupted with a chilling certainty.

"Can you heal me?" I asked.

"I've been trying since you showed up," the healer replied with a slight shake of her head.

That made me cringe.

Gratte had told me tons of stories about Band-Aid curing everything from severe burns to mild cases of death. I've used incurable poisons before—stuff so strong that even a healer couldn't undo its effects. Until now, I've never heard of an untraceable variant.

"It's a designer toxin," she explained with mild awe. "The shit's bonded to your DNA so perfectly that it's tricked your immune system into accepting it. Someone custom-made this just for you."

"Might be why your goggles can't spot it," Diglet suggested. "The stuff's part of you."

"That follows," Band-Aid nodded. "If I had to guess, there's a chemical leash involved."

Few of my enemies would bother with a chemical leash. They'd simply end me with an incurable poison, cover their tracks, and be done with it. Chemical leashes were used to control someone. In my case, if I stayed on my would-be killer's good side, I'd get a pseudo-cure. While not as good as the real thing, it would keep me alive. Pseudo-cures had to be administered on a regular basis; say, every few weeks or so.

If I missed a dose, I died.

"What would you do in my shoes?" I asked.

"Switch bodies or put your mind in a robot," Band-Aid half-joked as she opened her brown eyes. "You need to find out what this stuff is. Do that and maybe—maybe—I can put you in touch with someone who could reverse-engineer a real cure for you."

"If this is a chemical leash, there's a pseudo-cure," I said as I started to leave. "How long before I'll need that next dose?"

The healer paused for a thoughtful moment.

"Three days. Tops."

"If I miss that dose, what symptoms will I face?" I asked.

The healer looked up at me with a hint of pity.

"None," Band-Aid replied. "You'll simply black out and never wake up again."

CHAPTER SIX

I'm gonna cure myself.

Then I'm gonna kill whoever did this and make their kids watch. The most likely suspects would've been the ArgoKnights . . . and Juanita. As I flew home, my mind drifted her way. One hell of a cook, we dined at her place on the regular over the last two months. Roughly about the time I was poisoned with a chemical leash. I could almost hear Teke's voice in my head screaming at how fucking stupid I was to fall for a honeypot. What I couldn't believe was that ArgoKnights were behind this!

It all started straightforward enough.

During my first months as a do-gooder, I had a stash of 80's-era gadgets. Looted from an old ArgoKnight Way Station, most of the old tech still worked. The flight collar around my neck was part of that treasure trove. The annoying thing was that I had used up/bartered most of that tech within three months. Afraid of doing business with a marked-for-death guy like me, none of my old gadget vendors would even return my calls.

I hired some middlemen and started setting up black market supply lines. But the tech I needed was way too expensive. Then Grace came to me with an offer. She'd pay for my gadgets and plug me into a steady source of reliable threat intel. In exchange, I'd fight the good fight. When I pressed her for details, the psi-hacker simply said that her pals were ArgoKnights.

I didn't believe her at first. In their prime, the ArgoKnights were the world's largest hero team. Idealistic and noble, they inspired dozens of lesser teams to make the world a better place. The fuckers had 174 full-time heroes and a thousand Support Staff, some of whom were supers.

The heroes did the heavy lifting throughout the world, fighting evil and saving lives. The Support Staff were experts in various fields. They kept the ArgoKnight machine running by gathering intel and providing logistical support for the heroes and their hundreds of Way Station bases.

During *Clean Sweep,* most of the world's villains (myself included) teamed up and killed those do-gooder assholes. When the smoke cleared, the ArgoKnights were decimated. Street rumor was that the Support Staff, who manned their posts to the end, were also wiped out.

I found it hard to believe there were any survivors . . . or that they'd want to work with me. While not an ArgoKnight herself, Grace had earned their trust—and mine—through her actions. She vouched for them. I also had to admit that their intel led me to the HydroNemesis bomb last October. Simply because I couldn't save the world on my own, I accepted Grace's offer.

A few days later, they put me on to Juanita Torrez.

A natural-born super, she worked out of Pillar City. Before she came to town, Juanita was somebody else. To stay alive, she had to change her identity the same way I once did: new face, name, DNA, and an ironclad cover history. These days, her street name was Gunrack. While she was smart enough to build super weapons from scratch, Juanita's main claim to fame was testing them.

We hit it off from day one. Even Lia liked her.

It just didn't make sense, though! Juanita and her pals were in the same boat I was. The world was at stake. Lunatic bastards were coming out of the woodwork, thrilled with the idea of a world without super heroes. If I went down, they'd have to find some other chump(s) to pick up the slack. The problem was that every super hero I knew of was either dead, missing, or on the take.

Our arrangement was simple enough. The ArgoKnights found the threats and supplied the resources. I stepped into harm's way and (repeatedly) saved the world. Granted, I knew the Support Staff were sneaky fucks—but this?! Slipping a chemical leash on an ally was lower than low. It was at *my* level.

My mind snapped to the present as my building loomed ahead of me. In my anger, I told my flight collar to head home instead of the lair entrance. The damned thing had flown me right to the building's front doors. Eh, fuck it.

"Land," I commanded.

The collar set me down at the front entrance, where Lou Favinccio stood vigil. In his late 50's, the polite little man wore his red-and-black doorman's uniform (complete with hat and overcoat). The guy looked harmless enough to be a tailor or even have his own kids' show.

In reality, Lou used to kill people for a now-defunct Sicilian mob. I hired him last summer to handle difficult contracts for the firm. The deal was that I relocated him and his family to Canada, along with new papers and generous pay. In return, he'd put in a few years of high-end murder for me.

Lou was on his fifteenth victim when my firm collapsed. Most of my mercs abandoned me when I got stuck with Community Service. Not Lou. Seeing as I kept up my end of the deal, he insisted on keeping his for another year or two.

At first, I didn't trust him. Anyone could've gotten to him or his family, and then flipped his loyalties against me. Still, I needed a flesh-and-blood security unit to keep an eye on Lia. That's why I took a gamble on Lou—with failsafes built-in should he ever sell me out. I made it a point to have him augmented too. Nothing fancy: simply a psi-shield and a high-end combat symbiote. The former would protect his mind. The latter would make him very hard to kill.

"Good evening, Mr. Cly," Lou tipped his hat with a warm smile as he opened the door for me.

"Lou," I gruffly acknowledged him.

I entered the old-style lobby, which looked so innocent with its restored white marble flooring and matching columns. With the press of a button, it could become a high-density death trap capable of wiping out one hundred hostiles.

I headed for the stairs.

"Sir, is everything alright?" Lou's accented voice asked through my mouth radio.

Being my head of security, Lou had access to the frequency. Still, he rarely used it.

"Not even close, Lou," I replied as I entered the stairwell.

"Would it have anything to do with the Triad shooters in your loft, sir?"

I stopped mid-step.

"Excuse me?"

"A four-man team teleported into your loft roughly a half-hour ago," he reported.

I closed my eyes and groaned.

All the shit I've been through. The wars and horrors I've faced. It figures that I'd end up dead because of a semi-literate pimp with gold braces. Harlot must've gotten wind of my involvement in Wabbit's death. Head of all Wung Triad operations in Pillar City, the psychic "dragon lady" never did like me much. She apparently decided not to let his death go unanswered.

"Based on their gear, were they out to kill or capture me?" I asked.

"Judging from their op tech?" Lou assessed. "I'd venture that they were ready for either."

"Any survivors?" I asked, certain that Lou had killed them all, which would only worsen the situation with the Wungs.

"They're all alive, sir."

I exhaled an audible sigh of relief. "Consider your Christmas bonus tripled, Lou. Where are they now?"

"On the roof, sir."

"Thank you, Lou," I smiled. "I'll take it from here."

"Very good, sir."

A few seconds after "Lou" broke contact, I realized I was in a different sort of trap. The way this night was going, I was more paranoid than normal (which was why I had taken the stairs).

Here's the thing—Lou never called me "sir."

It was always "Mr. Cly."

Always.

I had to assume the Triad ambush team would know if I hit my panic button. Somehow, they had slipped past Lou, the rest of his team, and my expensive security arrangements. Worse, they had tapped into my encrypted radio chatter. Lastly, I knew my guys. When it came to intruders, they didn't take prisoners—not with Lia's safety at stake.

I continued upward.

The bogus message said four hostiles. Twelve-plus made more sense. I kept my stride easy and thoughtful, fairly certain that they had eyes on me (either psychic or technological). They must've spent months studying my security layout, picking out vulnerabilities, and then setting up this plan. The balls it took to fake the radio chatter impressed me. The brilliance of steering me toward the roof, where a sniper team could pick me off at leisure, was right out of my old playbook.

Guess I had to change the game a little . . .

About a half-hour later, the Triad shooters breached my loft.

Took 'em long enough. I was propped up in my bed, still in costume. After a ten-minute wait, they had to have known that I was on to them. Still, I figured that they weren't going to simply breach. They'd be cautious enough to request instructions before going to their Plan B.

While they scurried about, I popped some corn and started watching *Dredd* on my plasma screen. I then (discreetly) left a live screecher grenade on the kitchen counter. Barely the size of a bean, the olive-hued gadget would activate with the press of a detonator (like the one built into my utility sash).

In addition, I pitched an ice disc at my bedroom door. The pale blue, coin-shaped explosive hit the floor and exploded into a translucent wall of white ice. Thicker than a bank vault and twice as tough, it would keep out a breach team for a while. Years ago, I had my bedroom windows bricked over and lined with hyper-alloys. Between the walls and the ice barrier, the screecher grenade wouldn't impair me.

As the Triad shooters blew in my bullet-resistant living room windows, I realized that they didn't show up on my goggles' sensors. Stealth tech was involved—or maybe super powers. That's how I'd have done it.

I reached under the utility sash and pressed a button. The grenade's sudden, piercing shriek was so loud that it actually cracked the ice wall. Aside from inflicting sonic agony, it bombarded the loft with sonar waves. All of a sudden, my goggles could pick up sixteen sonar signatures. Dressed in SWAT-style attire, they were dropping like Asian flies. Even muffled, the damned weapon made me cringe.

The shattered glass and the screecher's wail would definitely alert Lou and his guys. Assuming they weren't dead or incapacitated, they'd get here double-quick. Hell, they might even see some action. I pulled one of my burner phones and dialed Harlot's personal number. She picked up on the second ring.

"Y'know, Harlot, you could've just called me if you wanted to talk," I shouted over the screecher grenade.

"Turn off the device," Harlot's voice demanded with a slight Mandarin accent.

Annoyed by the noise, I tapped the detonator button again. The grenade went silent.

"What was that?" I chuckled. "Couldn't hear you over the noise."

Harlot was quiet on the other end. I'd wager that she was stifling every Mandarin-language profanity in her pretty little head. When she finally spoke, her low tone promised me a sinister and painful death.

"Before I collect your head, my only question is, 'Why?'" Harlot asked.

"Hold on a sec," I said.

Phone in my left hand, I put a handful of popcorn in my mouth and loudly chewed as I rolled out of bed. With my right hand, I casually pulled an incendiary pellet from my utility sash. I then carefully flicked the mustard yellow sphere at the ice wall. On impact, it burned a tunnel through the obstacle—just like it was designed to. Steam hissed and swirled into my room. Some of my floor was scorched. The tunnel it made was about five feet high, which forced me to crouch a bit. I carefully walked out, and then rose to my full height.

"Sorry about that," I apologized. "Now, what the hell are you talking about?"

"You violated your Community Service," she asserted. "Tell me why."

"No I didn't," I grinned as I entered the hallway and stepped over a four-man squad.

I couldn't see their faces underneath the tear gas masks, metal helmets, and fancy goggles. Still alive, they packed more weapons than I did. I took a moment to wonder which of these poor idiots were supers. Their level of tech might've partially shielded them from such things as flash-bang grenades. Too bad screecher grenades were so much worse. Having blown out their eardrums, I should feel guilty about this.

I really should.

"What's with the breach team, Harlot?"

"You killed one of my associates."

"Bullshit!" I scoffed. "Who'd I allegedly kill, Harlot?"

I played coy, hoping to God that Harlot (with her accent) would say his fucking name.

"A pimp named Wabbit," she replied.

Needless to say, I laughed at her. Hard. Loud. The type of ridicule-laden laughter that would only make her hate me just a bit more. Lou and his five-man backup team (finally) kicked in the door. Dressed in doormen uniforms, they looked around, ready for anything. While the rest of my bodyguards had guns raised, Lou didn't bother. His glare could kill way better than bullets.

I covered my phone's mouthpiece and whispered, "Show them out. Alive."

Lou reluctantly nodded and snapped his fingers. Four of the shooters assumed an overwatch posture, while the fifth, Sal, lowered his weapon. He was a telekinetic, which came in handy during times like this.

The Triad shooters slowly floated off the floor, caught in the grip of Sal's power.

"Sorry about your guys," I said, surprised that I had stopped laughing at Harlot. "Tell ya' what: why don't I swing by and we'll sort this out like civilized villains?"

"Do you really think you can talk your way out of this?" Harlot scoffed.

"Don't see why not," I replied, heading for the kitchen. "I didn't kill him and you know it."

"And why should I believe you?" Harlot asked.

"Simple," I shrugged, as I picked up the screecher grenade and stuck it back into my utility sash. "In the nine-plus years you've known me, when was the last time I lied to you?"

Dead silence on the other end.

"Be here by dawn," came her blunt reply.

"I'll leave your guys out back, in case you—"

Click.

That was rude.

"How'd they get passed us?" Lou asked with a shamed frown.

"Months of planning," I mused as I reached into the cookie jar and pulled out a fistful of shelled pistachios. "Run a perimeter sweep and disable any devices they've planted."

Lou nodded, his face a mask of resolve. The Sicilian had kept plenty of my enemies at bay, especially when I had that huge bounty on my head. In his six months on the job, these unlucky bastards were the first ones to slip past him. He was embarrassed.

"What of Harlot?" Lou asked. "Should I return the favor?"

I grinned a tempted grin. "Let's hope it doesn't come to that, Lou."

CHAPTER SEVEN

I stepped into my lair and put Grace on the big screen. Aside from the part about being poisoned, I brought her up to speed. After I finished the briefing (and the pistachios), the psi-hacker gave me a look that screamed "you-lunatic-dumbass." Grace was still parked in front of that fucking brick wall. Part of me wondered if she had even taken a piss since we last talked.

"Maybe you should go missing, Cly," Grace hinted with concern.

"Why?" I asked with just enough fake innocence to annoy her.

"I dunno," Grace shrugged. "Maybe it's because you've just pissed off two of the most dangerous mobs on the planet."

God, my back was killing me!

"I don't run," I achingly replied as I grabbed a three-legged high stool and sat down.

She stared at me like I had just told her the Earth was flat.

"I've got this, Grace. Don't worry," I assured her. "Now, what about the girls?"

"I routed them to a safe house," Grace replied. "They're making Juliette some new identity papers as we speak."

"How long before it's done?" I asked.

"Midnight your time," she replied after a second of calculation. "Anywhere and Pinpoint will have their backs until the smoke clears."

Both former mercs of mine, Grace hired them a few days after my firm went under. These days, Pinpoint and Anywhere served as Grace Lexia's security detail.

She paid them well and they've saved her life on a handful of occasions.

In a firefight, Pinpoint could gun down a ten-man breach team inside of five seconds. During that interval, Anywhere (pussy that he was) would teleport away—hopefully with the ladies in tow.

They'd keep Lia safe.

I nodded my approval. Once I got Malcolm to safety, I'd finish my patrol and then go deal with Harlot. Grace promised to keep me updated on Lia. After the psi-hacker broke contact, I stood up and stretched. The beating the magslinger laid down on me was worthy of painkillers.

The lair's rear proximity alarm chimed, much like a doorbell. When Gratte's people built my lair, they designed this feature so that I'd know if anyone was lurking outside of my sewer exit. I headed over to the door controls, hit a few buttons, and an image popped up.

Juanita Torrez (a.k.a., Gunrack) calmly waited in the darkened tunnel.

Tonight, she wore a gray cotton duster, black-and-gray digicam fatigue pants, black combat boots, and a white sweater. Nestled between her B-cups was an ornate bronze cross that Gunrack claimed brought her luck. On her back was an old beige rucksack. She once told me it was a souvenir from her pre-ArgoKnight days, when she was an Army sniper. Her custom-made auto-pistol rested against her right thigh. The holster was strapped, which meant that she wasn't expecting trouble.

At forty-one, the short-haired Latina's muscled frame bordered on voluptuous (not that I minded). A bit taller than me, Gunrack's face was a tough kind of beautiful. A purple doo rag was wrapped around her short-cropped black hair. She had a new piercing; a silver loop through her lower-left lip. Gunrack didn't bother with makeup, perfume, or most of the other feminine touches. In terms of personality, she had a no-nonsense bluntness that made it easy to trust her.

I loved her. Told her as much and even meant it (not that it changed anything). When this was over, I'd kill her . . . simple as that. For now, I opted to play ignorant. Once the Support Staffers knew that I was aware of their scheme, they'd try to take me out. Before things reached that point, I needed to find a cure.

Time to bullshit.

I pressed a white button. The exit tunnel's round metal door slid aside.

"Hey sugar thighs," I grinned with an aching weariness that I didn't have to fake.

"You look awful," Gunrack winced as she studied me from the doorway. "What happened?"

"Someone tenderized me with a car."

"Foreign or domestic?" Gunrack joked as she stepped into my lair.

"Heavy," I muttered as I sealed the door with the press of a button.

Gunrack leaned in and kissed my right cheek.

"Maybe you should take the rest of the night off," she purred into my ear. "I could give you one of my whirlwind massages."

That got a smile out of me. She gave me one of those on my last birthday. Best sex I ever had. It started on my bed and ended up in the lair. She cracked a rib. I almost lost a back tooth.

Should've filmed it.

Gunrack closely looked me over more and realized that I wasn't joking about the car.

"Seriously, Cly, you all right?" she asked with a frown.

"Nothing a few years of sleep won't cure," I replied, shifting my demeanor into all-business mode. "What brings you by?"

Gunrack unslung her rucksack and dropped it on the table. Filled (as usual), she made sure that it would stay upright, and then looked my way.

"Thought I'd save you a gadget run," she said.

The backstabbing cunt sat across from me on one of the table's four high stools. Then she took a deep breath—like she had some major news.

"And, uh, the Section Chiefs want to meet."

I raised an eyebrow.

Since they were formed, the ArgoKnights were an egalitarian outfit. They shied away from picking a leader(s) because more heads were better than few. Those members with influence, charisma, or even seniority didn't hold sway. Nope, these heroes ran their outfit based on facts, regulations, and a simple moral compass.

No one strayed from this because it was woven into their psi-training. This kept common organizational woes (like infighting or cliques) to a bare minimum without turning everyone into blind-loyalist types. To them, any problem could be solved. A decision was right or wrong, wise or stupid. Add in the ArgoKnight rules and regulations . . . and *voila!* Solutions would emerge. This methodology was surprisingly effective— but also predictable.

In the end, that's how we beat them.

Having superior numbers, the first wave of crooks simply went on a synchronized global crime spree. They robbed, stole, kidnapped, and flat-out wreaked havoc. Even though they were the world's largest hero group, the ArgoKnights' resources were spread way too thin. This narrowed their options and made them vulnerable.

Then the second wave hit.

Made up of cutthroat bastards (like my mercs), we ambushed them while they were saving the day. The heroes saw it coming. They could've dropped what they were doing, coordinated a counterattack, and (maybe) beaten us. Instead, they sacrificed their lives to protect the innocent and died like good little heroes.

After *Clean Sweep,* Gunrack explained that the surviving ArgoKnights and Support Staffers elected a three-person leadership council. Dubbed the "Section Chiefs," they were tasked with rebuilding the organization. Only active members knew their names or faces, which made sense. Gunrack assured me that their roles were temporary. Supposedly, once the ArgoKnights were up and running again, they'd go back to their old framework.

What the fuck did they want with me?

"A new threat?" I asked as I leaned against the table.

"No," Gunrack smiled, her legs swinging back-and-forth. "You're being granted probationary access. They wanted to discuss terms."

My eyes narrowed with suspicion.

"After *Clean Sweep,* don't your pals hate me?" I asked.

"A few," she admitted. "But, after you saved the world a few times, even they had to admit that you've proven yourself."

I crossed my arms. "They wanna make me Support Staff?"

"No," Gunrack replied with a shake of her head and a slight smile. "You'd be an ArgoKnight: the first of many new heroes they plan to recruit."

My frown deepened.

This wasn't making sense. Why give me probationary status at all? That level of access would allow me to know names, safe house locations, and other sensitive information. I could easily smash their operations with that much inside knowledge. Right now, I had minimal intel on their organization, which I actually preferred.

In their shoes, I might've mentioned the chemical leash and dangled the pseudo-cure over my head. Such measures could be effective. In the old days, I practically swore by them. Instead, the ArgoKnights were offering me a place at the table. Maybe the chemical leash was their way of keeping me honest.

"You don't look thrilled," Gunrack frowned.

We've had this argument before. I wasn't a hero and never would be. I was a die-hard crook whose business just happened to be fighting crime. Community Service kept the mobs off my back. Grace paid my business expenses. I've also earned billions off the bad guys I've taken down. Some called it "looting" but I saw it as . . . "confiscating" dangerous assets for the public good. With virtually no overhead to worry about, I made more money as a crime fighter than I ever did as a fixer. This would end if I became an ArgoKnight.

Then came the other drawbacks.

I'd have to be all "good" and shit. The mobs would definitely kill me. Worse, the ArgoKnights didn't kill people unless it was the only option. In fact, they had more rules and regulations than any bureaucracy in human-fucking-history.

"Are you finally throwing out the ArgoKnight playbook?" I asked, knowing full well what she'd say.

"Of course not," Gunrack replied. "Those rules are necessary. Without them, the original ArgoKnights would've fallen apart decades ago."

She had a point. In these dark times, common guidelines were a necessity when recruiting (honest) heroes. They'd have both a moral and operational platform from which to function. Of course, that could also become a liability. If the rules hadn't changed, then they could be "gamed," just like any other system of regs. When villains (like me) literally had copies of the ArgoKnight rulebook, it was time to write a new one.

"It's a bad idea, 'Rack."

"Why?" she pressed, bothered that I never saw this her way.

"Joining the Support Staff's risky enough," I argued. "Stepping out into the open with a hero team's like leading lambs to slaughter, regardless of their powers. They'd have to work out of the shadows."

"That's not how ArgoKnights do things—"

"Then adapt," I interrupted her. "In case you haven't noticed, there's no public outcry for super heroes anymore."

"We could change that, Cly," Gunrack insisted. "The villains turned the public against us last time. It won't happen again."

I just kept shaking my head.

"It won't save you from the most dangerous power of them all," I warned her.

"What? Money?" she scoffed. "We can counter that."

I shook my head. So brilliant and yet so naïve . . .

"Money's one of the top five most dangerous super powers," I patiently explained. "The ArgoKnights had tons of assets before *Clean Sweep*. Did it save them? No."

Gunrack was starting to get pissed. She hopped off her stool and began to pace around the table, putting it between us.

"Okay, Cly, what's the most dangerous power of them all?"

"Ruthlessness," I evenly replied. "The ability to do whatever it takes makes you both unpredictable and feared. If the ArgoKnights go 'old-school' they'll be dead in a year, tops."

She was fuming as I thoughtfully eyed the ceiling.

"Hell! Since 2011, any super who's stepped out in costume's ended up dead within weeks—except for me."

My girlfriend/would-be killer took a cleansing breath. Maybe that was the idea behind this whole chemical leash scenario. I survived and they wanted to put their stamp on my success. A new class of "leashed" villain/hero type, perhaps.

"So you're not interested?"

"When you guys decide to be ruthless, give me a call," I replied, backing away. "Besides, I'll be dead in three days."

The bitch knew about the poison. Gunrack's confused reaction proved it. She thought I was talking about my three-day life span. Instinctively, her right hand drifted toward the auto-pistol. Maybe she figured I'd kill her right then and there. She thought wrong . . . I'll kill her when I'm cured.

I defused the situation by reaching for my Marlboros.

"Why won't you last three days?" Gunrack asked with narrowed eyes.

"You heard about Dr. Wabbit?" I asked.

"Grace sent me an update," Gunrack gave me a curious frown. "That's what you're worried about?"

"Shouldn't I be?" I replied. "You know how the Wungs are about their franchisees. I'm dead meat, 'Rack."

Her posture relaxed as I lit up. Deep in thought, Gunrack walked over next to me. She rifled through her rucksack for a moment, and then sighed as she looked my way.

"I don't think Harlot's coming after you, Cly."

"Tell that to the sixteen-member kill team she just sent my way," I replied.

Gunrack sighed as she pulled out five plastic boxes of spare gadgets.

"Are they dead?"

"Nah," I replied.

"Then you need to get off the grid," she muttered.

"Not happening," I replied. "I'm going to wrap up a few errands and then meet with her."

"On *The Depravity*?!" Gunrack balked, looking over at me like I was fucking nuts. "You do know that's a one-way trip, right?"

"I've haggled under worse conditions," I confidently replied. "I could use a favor, though."

"Name it," Gunrack shrugged as she continued to unpack.

I reached into my mouth and pulled out the mouthpiece radio. I dropped the saliva-drenched gadget onto the table.

"Her people hacked my comms."

Gunrack exhaled a litany of Spanish profanities on the tip of her limber tongue. The gal was sexy when she swore.

"Those Triad fuckers flipped *my* tech?!" she scowled. "Are you sure?"

"One of 'em did a decent impersonation of Lou," I explained. "Had I not been on the ball, I'd be dead right now. That means . . ."

"They've bypassed your building's security," she nodded, understanding my request. "I trust that you'll want a floor-by-floor sweep?"

"Fuck yeah."

"Mind if I bring some people in?" she asked. "It'll go faster that way."

"I do, actually," I replied with a gentle smack on her generous ass. "Coordinate with Lou or he might get paranoid and kill you."

I didn't trust the Support Staff and she knew it. During *Clean Sweep*, my guys went after bounties on fourteen ArgoKnights and a few dozen Support Staffers. Some we killed. Others we captured and sold to eager buyers. A few even got away from us (only to get killed by someone else). In the end, their surviving ArgoKnight pals hated my guts.

"Toss me your Glocks, then," Gunrack said as she pulled out a pair of guns. "Can't have you running off to certain death with just any old handguns."

She handed over the new guns. Both weapons looked like Glocks, just heavier. My goggles scanned the weapons, which were made of a metal I couldn't pronounce. It also picked up weird energy wavelengths coming off them.

I didn't reach for my guns, which I had left at *Smitty's*.

"Where are your Glocks?" Gunrack asked.

"I lost them," I muttered as I took her guns and holstered them.

She started to ask what happened and then thought better of it.

"What do these do?" I asked.

"They'll kill whatever ails you," Gunrack replied with a pretty grin. "Gimme one."

I complied.

"You've tested this?" I asked. Some of the shit she played with worked great. Others didn't.

A bit insulted, Gunrack muttered something under her breath as she reached into her rucksack and pulled out a ripe banana. She flung it toward a vacant patch of floor space, waited for it to stop moving, and then zapped it with my new gun. The banana instantly turned into a small cloud of gray ashes.

"Hit any organic matter—animal, vegetable, or person—and it becomes ash."

"What about inanimate objects?" I asked.

She aimed at my concrete floor, fired, and left a fist-sized hole in it. No loud *boom* or messy cloud of shrapnel-like debris. Just a faint hum and then a hole. Gunrack handed the weapon back. I holstered it with enhanced respect.

"Whose guns are these?" I asked.

"Yours," Gunrack winked. "I was saving 'em for Christmas."

Funny. My present for her was an engagement ring with a platinum band and a $6 million emerald on top. I carried it in my coat, for luck. Note to self: hock it for something useful.

"Thanks," I replied, wondering if I'd have to use these fancy guns on her someday soon.

Gunrack opened the big boxes to reveal smaller ones, each containing the usual toys: gas bombs, explosives, truth serum injectors, etc. She even threw in a utility belt to wear over my gun belt. Gunrack slipped my radio into her pocket and then loaned me her wristcom. I wrapped the dark brown device around my left wrist. After picking out the gadgets best suited for a Triad visit, I put the utility belt on and checked my watch.

She took the hint and packed up her rucksack.

"Anything else I can do?" Gunrack asked.

"Sweep the bedroom last," I replied as I put the wristcom on my left wrist. "I left some new lingerie in your drawer."

Yep. The bitch had her own drawer. That's how serious things had gotten between us. I masked my hate with lust as I pulled her in and gave her a hard kiss on the lips. Gunrack moaned with mild pleasure and then gently pushed me away. I pulled my mask down.

"Be careful," she said with convincing concern on her face.

"You too," I nodded toward her sidearm. "Keep that gun close."

I led her toward the exit.

"Oh! Wait," Gunrack grinned as she pulled out a foil-wrapped hoagie.

Still warm, the scent made my mouth water. Every week, it was something different. Each hoagie recipe stunned my taste buds. This one smelled like chicken with some kind of sauce and . . . seasoned potato slices maybe?

My goggles tagged it as "safe" (as always). Of course, since she made these fucking goggles, Gunrack could've programmed them to ignore certain things— like the chemical leash or even the pseudo-cure. If administered properly, in a timely manner, I'd never know I had been poisoned. Gunrack slipped me one hoagie per week, one/more of which was probably my "dosage." That was how she was keeping me alive.

Hoagie in hand, I escorted Gunrack to the surface. Once I left her with Lou (at the main entrance) I pitched it into the first trash bin I saw. The hoagie might have a pseudo-cure in it, which could buy me another month of life. Or, they knew about Band-Aid's diagnosis and had decided to lace it with something new. As I walked along the sidewalk, passing pedestrians pointed and whispered. My masked face was known on these streets, which made my work easier . . . most of the time.

Band-Aid's offer, about her biochemist friend, crossed my mind. The problem was that I couldn't rely on her unknown contact. In four days, I'd have a tag on my toe. Reverse-engineering a cure (in my experience) took way longer than that—weeks, at least.

This would have to wait.

I tapped the flight collar and soared off toward the Jove Street stash house. Along the way, my thoughts drifted back to Malcolm O'Flernan. Leaving him there was a mistake. Once the O'Flernans tracked the kid down, they'd send their top killers. They might be good enough to get passed Band-Aid and kill everyone on the site. Grace could help the kid disappear. Getting him to her (with a pulse) could be tricky.

Less than twenty minutes later, I was relieved to find everyone safe and sound. Malcolm was on his feet now, still entranced. Speck sat on a stack of crates, with a high-intensity headlamp wrapped around her forehead. Like a surgeon, she "operated" on the kid's inhibitor collar. The collar's outer housing had been removed to reveal five different micro-detonators. I've never seen that many on a collar before. I looked down and raised an eyebrow at the tiny clumps of plastique at our feet.

Speck looked over and wiped some sweat from her brow.

"This is some tricky bomb work, Cly," she said.

"No shit. Recognize the handiwork?"

The lady shook her head and gave me a concerned look. "I can tell you that this thing's a modified Mark-10 inhibitor collar."

"I know that, Speck—"

"You don't waste one of these on your average super," she continued. "You stick it on God. This kid's power level must be somewhere near insane."

Speck paused and looked me in the eye.

"You sure you don't want me to put it back together?"

"It's deactivated?" I asked.

"Had to," Speck nodded. "It's the only way I could disarm the explosives. Once he recovers from the gas, nothing's holding his powers in check."

I sighed, almost wishing that I let the magslinger kill this kid.

"Did it come with a tracking chip?" I asked.

"No," Speck replied.

I looked at Malcolm's eyes, which weren't blue anymore. They were black (which was starting to freak me out a bit). I pulled a gray inhibitor grenade from my utility harness.

"Step back," I warned her. "I'll dose him with inhibitor mist until we can sort this out."

Speck looked relieved as we both moved away. The grenade had a twenty-foot blast radius (give-or-take). I readied my toss and then threw it.

Halfway toward Malcolm's chest, a large hand caught the grenade. My goggles abruptly warned me of the presence of a psychic entity—one I just happened to recognize. He looked a damned-lot like Seamus' older son, Connor. The curly-haired, redheaded Irish . . . "whatever" wore a smart beige suit, maroon shirt, and no tie.

Connor looked just as mid-twenties as the day he died, with a freckled charisma to his strong face. A ladies' man in his day, he relied on charm and forcefulness to get what he wanted. He was supposed to run the mob someday.

The grenade harmlessly went off with a muffled *boom.*

"Well! Isn't this a surprise?" Connor smiled as stray wisps of green inhibitor gas came out of his closed fist.

Speck moved up to my left, a gun in each hand. I looked around. The rest of Gratte's workers were slowly edging away; some went for their own guns and others toward the nearest exits. An awe-struck Band-Aid climbed out of her sub-basement. Connor slapped his hands together, getting rid of the grenade fragments. Completely unaffected, the entity walked over with a blue-eyed smile and an outstretched hand.

I had nothing in my arsenal to deal with this threat. Flesh-and-blood targets, yes. Tech-based enemies? No problem. Right now, I was looking at the black eyes of a living *thought.*

And it (no, *he*) wanted to shake hands.

CHAPTER EIGHT

Connor and I shook hands.

His grip was firm and his body language polite. We'd met before and swapped small talk, back when I was an up-and-comer. While we weren't friends, we weren't necessarily enemies either. As Connor released my hand, the goggles hit me with a tactical alert. The results flashed across my lenses . . . and they were goddamned frightening.

There was an Omega-level energy threat in the room.

Natural disasters didn't fall under this category. Neither would a zombie apocalypse or a limited nuclear exchange. An Omega-level threat was more like a super nova, black hole, or a planet-killing weapon. It was the type of nightmarish scenario where everything on Earth died (even the roaches).

The funny thing about this sensor reading was that Connor wasn't the source—Malcolm was! The drugged *kid* was throwing off massive amounts of psychic energy, which his dead father had (somehow) managed to tap into. If Connor wasn't careful, his son might actually explode—taking a hemisphere or two with him.

"That really you, Connor?" I asked with a slow grin.

"Down to the dick size," Connor grinned in reply, utterly ignoring Speck's guns, which were now aimed at his face.

I couldn't blame his confidence. Depending on what kind of entity he was, her bullets would either pass through his energy form or harmlessly bounce off it. Based on his firm handshake, my guess was on the latter.

"I think I liked you better in a suit, Cly," Connor teased.

"Times have changed since you . . . died," I replied with a curios frown. "You are dead, right?"

"That I am," Connor sighed, eyes darkening. "Death by car bomb is most unenjoyable."

"What about Angus?" I asked. "Did he make it out?"

"He's gone," the entity replied, his eyes mixed with sadness and anger.

"My condolences."

Oddly enough, I meant it.

The second oldest of Seamus' three kids, Angus O'Flernan was everyone's favorite son. The philanthropist of the family, he wasn't a crusading do-gooder but a realist; one who supported underdog causes that were vital but underappreciated. The clever young man had used the family's political muscle to generate support for various causes—from global women's rights to climate change. Hell! Angus even managed to pull donations out of my evil hide.

Connor and Angus were both in the same car when the bomb went off some ten years ago. After the bombing, Seamus spent years looking for those responsible. In fact, I was one of the many fixers he hired to aid in the search. Like everyone else, I wanted to know who killed them and why. In the end, we all came up blank. Whoever did this left nary a trace, which made sense.

After all, Seamus O'Flernan wasn't the forgiving type.

I thought back to Vincent Mockre, an ArgoKnight mole who earned a niche in the O'Flernan mob. Upon discovering Mockre's betrayal, Seamus had him snatched up. After a solid week of torture, the poor fool was the guest of honor at his own Irish wake, *while he was still breathing*. With a live band in the background, we watched Mockre get beaten almost to death, lose his tongue, and then get left to die in an airtight coffin.

I glanced over at Malcolm. Locked within his own mind, the poor kid simply stared off into space. His dad stood between us with a thin smile as he watched most of Gratte's team run away. Speck and Diglet stayed behind, along with Band-Aid and a few others.

Band-Aid's eyes were on Malcolm, her face a mask of frustration. A betting man might've thought she was trying to kill the kid with her abilities. The problem with that idea was that there was no fucking way the healer would get into the kid's mind. The Omega-level psychic bond (between father and son) was way out of her league. As long as it was up, she couldn't touch him.

"You're not a ghost, are ya?" I asked with a forced smile.

"Of course not!" the dead mobster laughed. "I'm simply a walking thought given shape."

I looked over at Malcolm, feigning ignorance.

"He saved you then?"

Connor nodded. "Even though my boy was a toddler at the time, we had a close bond. After the blast, I ended up trapped in the lad's head. I only found my way out last year."

"A psi-link?" I asked, still playing dumb.

He gave me another nod. "Lucky for me, Malcolm's psychic. A gift from his mother, I suppose."

For a moment, the dead O'Flernan looked very alive and equally sad.

"I hadn't planned on coming back here until Malcolm was a man," Connor admitted.

The entity looked around the site with freshly made decisions on his face.

"Guess I'll have to rethink things."

"What could you possibly want in Pillar City?" I asked, knowing full well why he was here.

Sure enough, Connor gave me a knowing grin.

"You know why I'm here," he scoffed. "There's blood to be spilled; lots of it, in fact."

"Whose?" I asked with genuine interest.

For a moment, Connor considered telling me. Then he shook his head.

"Sorry, Cly. This is a personal matter."

"Can I ask a favor, then?"

"Anything," Connor casually replied. "You saved my boy's life. That puts me in your debt."

"Avenge your murder and then get your son off the grid. He shouldn't have shit to do with the Irish mob."

Connor exploded into a fit of laughter, which echoed through the room for several seconds.

"He's an O'Flernan, Cly!" Connor proudly exclaimed. "He'll have everything to do with this mob because it's his fuckin' birthright!"

"What about going legit?"

"That wasn't bullshit," Connor replied. "I have big plans for the family—in time."

I took a diplomatic pause.

"Your son's too young to drink, drive, or even legally fuck," I argued. "What would Malcolm possibly know about running a multi-billion-dollar enterprise?"

"I'll back him," came his stubborn reply. "A bit of psi-training and he'll be just fine."

"It's a recipe for an all-out street war," I insisted. "Whether you or Deidre come out on top, the O'Flernan mob will suffer for it."

This is what sucked about being a "good guy."

As a fixer, I'd have happily bankrolled Connor's idiot scheme, just to watch the O'Flernans tear themselves apart. Now, I had to worry about innocent civilians and shit. More importantly, I had to keep the kid out of harm's way. If Malcolm O'Flernan died while that psi-link was active . . . *BOOM.* No more human race.

The entity folded his brawny arms and thoughtfully regarded me.

"So you think I should just get my revenge and let Malcolm live the quiet life, eh?"

"It isn't doomed to end in tears," I replied. "If he's off the grid, your only child has a chance at a ripe old age and grandkids. Most importantly, the O'Flernan name will endure. At the end of the day, isn't that the goal of any father?"

That last part made Connor flinch a bit. I stepped past the entity and looked down at Malcolm.

"You go down this path and the kid'll never be safe."

The entity gently chewed his lower lip for a moment. Then he looked me dead in the eye.

"No," said Connor. "I won't stop now."

I started to speak but he interrupted with a raised right hand.

"Let me finish," Connor sighed, his expression darkening. "While we're talking about vengeance, there's the issue of you killing my *da!*"

His wicked left haymaker came out of nowhere. Blocked from the light, I was barely fast enough to duck under it and skip back. Speck backed off as I circled away from her and assumed a boxing stance.

"So you want to play 'hero' eh?" the entity grinned as he stepped toward me.

Guard up, Connor expected me to treat this like a normal fight.

It wasn't though.

I couldn't hurt him with brute force. Also, he might be stronger than me. Bothered by this reality, I rushed in and knocked Connor off his feet with a left uppercut.

Super strength or not, he didn't weigh that much. The entity landed face-first and actually laughed.

"When'd you get so strong, Cly?!" Conner asked as he started to rise.

I was too busy with the running punt (to his ribs) to answer. The kick sent Connor partway through a far wall. Thirty feet away was a good, safe distance. I plucked another ice disc and flung it his way. Connor was back on his feet, without a hint of pain, when the gadget hit him right in the chest. The disc's gas cloud encased the startled entity in a near-instant block of ice.

Diglet nervously walked up behind me.

"Will that hold him?" he stupidly asked.

"You're welcome to stay and find out," I replied, my eyes on the ice block. "Or you can run the fuck away."

Gratte's other folks took the hint and ran off. Diglet started to leave—

"Wait!" Speck shouted as tiny cracks began to appear in the ice. "The inhibitor collar! Put it back together!"

I frowned at the disassembled device and then over at Diglet. The quasi-speedster used his hands more for digging than for precision device repair. Still, they were faster than mine. Also, as one of Gratte's staff, he had been psi-trained do all kinds of technical shit.

"Do you know how?" I asked.

Connor's right fist punched through the ice. He'd be loose in seconds. Speck half-dragged a reluctant Diglet to the stool and sat him down. The speedster hastily looked over the inhibitor collar and the tools she had used to take it apart.

"Maybe," he nodded. "I'll need thirty seconds."

Connor busted out with a grunt of effort, the smile gone from his face.

"You've got twenty!" I said as I rushed off.

Connor picked up a shovel as I ran toward him.
The O'Flernan twirled it in his right hand. Normally, I'd
pull the wakizashi and slice him open. The problem
here was that the impervium blade might rupture his
energy form and blow us all to hell.

Fearing the worst, I closed in barehanded.

Then I made one itsy mistake. A regular guy
swinging a shovel one-handed would be cake to dodge.
The tool was heavy and slow to wield. Anyway, I
figured my souped-up reflexes would save me. The
problem here was that Connor was strong enough to
swing that fucker like a damned rapier.

I dodged the first two swipes only to get clocked by
the third. The mistreated shovel shattered across my left
jaw. Knocked off-balance, I hit the ground and rolled to
my feet. My mask soaked up most of the damage. I was
okay. A bit embarrassed, I scowled and hopped up to
my feet—

—just in time to get a kick to the nuts.

The entity punted me into the ceiling with such
force that I barely felt the ceiling or the hard landing that
followed. Just my poor, achy balls. There were some
things from which a costume just couldn't protect you.

"Now *that* had to hurt!" Connor teased as he
stomped on my face.

The brutal impact drove my head into the floor.
With a sadistic grin, Connor pulled my mask and
goggles off, just to see my suffering. Too dazed to stop
him, I could only look up as he rolled me onto my back.
With my mask off, the surrounding lights sapped my
powers like air exiting a balloon. Within seconds, I was
a mere human again. Another hit to the face and I'd be a
goner.

Connor knelt on my chest, pinning me with ease
and savoring this moment. He cocked back his right fist,
eager to turn my skull into abstract art. I glanced beyond

the bastard. Diglet was hard at work; his hands and arms moved inhumanly fast. Without my help, they wouldn't be able to collar the fucker.

"Too bad you're not a fixer anymore Cly," Connor replied as his left hand found my throat and began to squeeze. "You'd have been useful."

The flight collar began to give in under the force of his grip. Hardly able to see straight, all I could do was die—

A cluster of bullets harmlessly ricocheted off the entity's torso. Connor turned and gave Speck a mocking laugh.

"You've got some stupid friends, Cly!"

The thing was that Speck wasn't trying to kill him.

"Does he now?" Speck asked as she pointed both her guns at Malcolm.

Oh. Shit.

"Get off him—now!" she yelled.

Connor's jaw dropped at the implications. He was sharp enough to figure that his life was tied to his son's. What he didn't know was that a bullet through Malcolm's head might kill us all. Worse, it looked to me that Speck wasn't bluffing. To her, whacking the kid would've been the logical way to end this threat.

The entity slowly let go of my neck. Just as he started to rise, there was a sudden implosion of air. Connor spun around just in time to collect a brutal punt to the face. The entity slammed through another far wall and into an abandoned bathroom. Lia stepped into my line of sight and glanced over her left shoulder.

"Evac in ten seconds!" she yelled. "Ten seconds!"

There was another implosion of air. Through my blurring vision, I saw Anywhere appear behind Speck and Diglet.

Imagine taking a short, skinny race horse jockey and giving him god-like teleportation powers. That was

Anywhere. Dressed head-to-toe in black tactical fatigues, he wore a black balaclava mask, a Kevlar-lined utility vest, ArgoKnight sensor goggles, and a black military-style helmet. Anywhere only carried a double-barreled shotgun for intimidation purposes. At times, I wondered if he even loaded the damned thing.

Still, when it came to moving tons of mass from Point A to B, Anywhere was top shelf. The teleporter simply needed a mental image of his destination and he could go there. Granted, Anywhere's power had limits. To get us out of here, for example, we all had to be within ten feet of him.

Right now, we weren't.

"Hey!" Diglet yelled, as the trio appeared near me. "I'm workin' here!"

"You don't understand!" Speck added. "He's not finished—"

"He is now," Anywhere interrupted as he teleported them away.

Band-Aid was running toward us as Connor stepped through the hole and gave Lia an evil glare.

"Should I try the tanglenets?" she asked me. "Or the psi-beam projector, maybe?"

Her armor's tanglenets could stop a charging rhino but not this guy. None of her armor's non-lethal weaponry could restrain him. The armor's psi-beam projector (one of her more lethal weapons) could fry the mind of anyone it hit. It might—just might—kill this fucker . . . along with the rest of the planet.

"Neither," I told her.

Anywhere collected Band-Aid in mid-stride and brought her in too. Only Malcolm remained, still staring off into space. Connor saw Anywhere appear next to his son. The entity's sneer switched to hot rage in a heartbeat.

"Touch him and I'll fucking kill you!" Connor bellowed.

Anywhere hesitated for a moment and then teleported away with Malcolm. The entity broke into a charge with nothing but murder in his eyes. Lia looked around for any stragglers. Connor had covered half the distance between us when she gave Anywhere the nod.

Then we were gone.

CHAPTER NINE

We appeared in Meadows Park under a streetlight.

By day, it was a poor man's Central Park with plenty of ways to have nice, clean fun. Too bad the park wasn't so safe after dark. By this time of night, only scum or fools came down here. As Lia gently set me down on a picnic table, I wondered which one I was.

"How bad?" Speck asked Band-Aid.

"Nothing I can't fix," the healer replied with a smirking glance at my groin. "Give me a minute."

Within seconds, my assorted injuries stopped hurting. I gave Band-Aid a grateful nod. Then I glanced over at Lia. "How'd you get here so fast?"

"Grace," she replied. "You wanted her on overwatch, remember?"

I was beginning to think Grace Lexia was tracking my every fucking move these days. She was still scared that I might go all "shadow monster" on the world. That made me wonder just how much the psi-hacker knew about this fucking chemical leash. Even if she wasn't in on the scheme, Grace had to know.

She had to know.

"Once Grace hacked Gratte's passive sensors," Anywhere added, "she saw what was happening and called us in."

I bit my tongue and looked convinced.

"Get that collar on him," I said as I heard my pelvic bone snap back into place. I carefully holstered the Colt, pleased that it came with us.

"That's what I was tryin' to tell ya'!" Diglet bitched. "I wasn't finished fixin' it! How do we shut him off now?!"

"No worries," Lia replied as a small needle slid out of her armor's left palm.

With that, my kid gently tapped Malcolm along his right carotid artery. Her armor came with three doses in each glove—one of Samir's ideas. Her doses were laced with Paucium. The heavy-duty inhibitor serum would negate Malcolm's abilities for the next 12 hours.

"We can't stay here," Speck said, bothered by our surroundings.

Even we weren't crazy enough to hang out here for too long. The destination was a good one, though. The kid's Omega-level power signature would shine like a Christmas tree—both on Jove Street and right here. The planet was swarming with satellites designed to track this kind of threat. Some belonged to governments. Others belonged to private-sector opportunists. Sooner or later, guys with sensors and guns would come around to investigate.

Better they stormed into a dangerous urban park than my loft.

"We left most of the background radiation behind us," Lia announced.

Diglet gently set the collar's two halves on the table next to me.

"Get me some tools and I'll finish the job," he lamely offered.

"Thanks, anyway," I told him.

"Don't mention it," Diglet replied.

I looked over at Anywhere. "You know what Glue looks like?"

The teleporter frowned for a moment and then nodded.

"Then get his ass down here. Now."

Anywhere gave me a two-fingered salute and then vanished.

"Band-Aid and Lia have overwatch," I said as I sat up, feeling much better. "Speck, you wanna stay or go?"

"You paying?"

"Of course," I smiled.

Speck paused to weigh the pros and cons of rolling with me. Then she shook her head.

"Maybe in the 90's, Cly," the shrinker replied with a reluctant smile. "Right now, I'm too young to die."

We shared a smile as Band-Aid stepped away from me.

"Likewise," the healer added. "This is out of my league."

"Thanks just the same, ladies," I replied.

A few seconds later, Anywhere reappeared with Glue. The kidnapper shouted in shock as he fell past the teleporter. My guess was that Glue had been sitting when he was snatched. I chuckled at his khaki shorts and tropical-style bowling shirt. Judging from his apparent lack of op tech, the hijacker might've been on a plane out of town.

Speck, Band-Aid, and Diglet headed over to Anywhere, eager to get the fuck away from this mess.

"Gratte's office?" Anywhere asked.

I nodded. Band-Aid gave me a strange smile before she disappeared with the others.

"What the fuck's going on?!" Glue barked. "Who the hell are you people?!"

Then he noticed me and got really angry. I hopped off the table while he got into my face, surprisingly unafraid.

"I thought we had an understanding, Cly!"

"That's before Connor O'Flernan popped out of his kid's mind and started slapping me around."

Glue's face twisted with disbelief as he looked over at Malcolm, who was still as rigid as a mannequin. The hijacker's eyes widened as he noticed the disabled inhibitor collar on the table.

"You took off the collar?!"

"Yeah, asshole," I smirked. "Care to tell me why you put it on him?"

"That was part of the arrangement," Glue replied. "I was instructed to buy a Mark-10 collar, rig it with explosives, and then leave it on him until the rendezvous. Now, if you don't mind, I'd like to get the fuck out of here!"

"Where was the rendezvous?" I asked him.

Glue shrugged. "Once I grabbed the kid, I tried to make contact with Ronns. Nothing."

I started to say something when the world changed.

One moment, I was normal. The next, I could sense . . . everything. The stink off a stray cat. The faint remnants of Glue's mediocre aftershave. The surrounding darkness didn't seem so dark. My senses were heightened again (an advantage I had lost months ago). Even though light was supposed to cancel my powers, I could feel them still working.

"You okay?" Lia asked.

"Yeah," I replied with a glance in Glue's direction. His adhesion power . . . I could see it!

My power gaze was back!

Band-Aid had (somehow) done this. She deserved a big, sloppy kiss—and a ton of cash—for this good deed. I bit back a smile. The healer managed to reactivate some of my old powers. The "how" of it could wait until tomorrow. The one thing I wouldn't do was tell the "ArgoFucks" about it.

That would be fair.

I put my mind back to the mess at hand. If Glue lost contact with Ronns, then the ex-Shepherd might be in trouble. Frankly, that didn't concern me. Right now, the Omega's psi-link was at the front of the line. I abruptly turned to Lia, annoyed that I had forgotten our arrangement.

"Sorry to give you orders, boss," I said with a smug grin. "This is your show, remember?"

Lia sighed within her armor. This scenario, as fucked up as it was, would give her some valuable field experience. It would be best if she ran the show. Lia paused to consider her options and then turned away from me.

"Grace, you still have eyes on the site?" Lia asked. "Good. Pipe it through to my armor."

A few seconds later, one holoimage erupted from the armor's chest plating. The square image coalesced into a real-time picture of Connor O'Flernan plowing through the front wall of the Jove Street site. The image switched to a perimeter sensor's POV.

The entity desperately looked around for a moment, and then started running off.

"Grace says that he's headed our way," Lia reported. "Putting you on speaker now."

"How do we stop him, Cly?" Grace asked through the armor.

Anywhere teleported in, looking a bit flustered.

"Gratte wants a word," he informed me.

"He'll have to wait," I replied. "Babysit the kid and watch our backs."

Anywhere nodded and moved next to Malcolm.

"How do we stop him, fearless leader?" I asked Lia.

I could hear whispered profanities come out of her helmet.

"A containment unit might work . . ." she theorized aloud.

"Most of them are under government lock-and-key," Grace cautioned. "Stealing them will be hard and stuffing Connor into one could be even harder."

Right on all counts.

"You and Connor were discussing a psi-link, right?" Lia asked me.

"Yeah," I nodded, pleased that she was on the right track.

"Cut the link and you cut his supply of psychic energy," she reasoned. "Given enough time, Connor would starve."

That's my girl.

"How long will that take?" Grace worriedly asked as we watched Connor run onto Jove Street.

The entity stopped at an intersection and flipped a passing car onto its passenger side. Connor hopped onto the driver's side of the black Lexus and ripped it clean off. Then he pitched the door and plucked out the driver (some terrified middle-aged guy). To everyone's surprise, Connor let the poor fucker run away. Then the entity righted the two-door car, got in, and drove off at high speeds.

"He could track a psi-link right to the kid," said a worried Glue, who turned toward Anywhere. "Get us out of here!"

"He'll find us wherever we go," Lia calmly replied. "Anywhere, you have a mind pill on you?"

I regarded my daughter with quiet pride.

"Never leave home without it," Anywhere smiled as he pulled one out of his utility harness.

The white gadget vaguely resembled an antacid tablet. When swallowed, the nanite-based pill would break down in the body and render the user resistant to mental powers for up to 24 hours. Combined with the Paucium injection, the mind pill might be good enough to break an Omega-level psi-link.

Lia cleverly crushed the mind pill in her left palm, so as to not choke the kid. Then, she poured the nanodust down Malcolm's throat. After an ordeal this bad, Malcolm O'Flernan had every right to stay zombified for a week. Instead, after a few seconds, the poor kid winced at the mind pill's awful taste. Fully aware again, he looked around at us with evident confusion.

"Where am I?" Malcolm asked with innocent blue eyes.

I started to say something when a bunch of someones howled off in the darkness. I could hear their breathing, fast-beating hearts, and crouching steps. There was also the stench of bad breath, body odor, and assorted intoxicants. They were junkies, most likely. Their addictions were so potent that they would try to mug anyone—even a group of armed supers.

"Grace, we need a safe house," Lia said, as the others anxiously looked around.

"Sending an image now," Grace replied.

Anywhere tapped his goggles.

"I see it," he confirmed with a relieved smile. "Gather 'round and let's get out of here."

We started to comply, when Lia gently took me by the arm.

"I need you here," she said with a low voice. "If anyone comes looking for Malcolm, I want him or her to find you first."

Lia had a point.

"Using your old man as bait?" I teased. "What's the world coming to?"

"You up to it?" she hesitantly asked.

I nodded as I glared at Glue.

"Squeeze him like a grape," I told her. "He knows something we can use."

"Plan to," Lia promised me. "I'll be in touch."

I gave her a reassuring nod before Anywhere whisked them away. In all the excitement, the inhibitor collar had been left behind. I scooped it up and put it into my coat. Then I sat on the picnic table and fired up a Marlboro.

I listened in on the distant whispering as the junkies argued about the wisdom of fucking with me. Without my mask, they could see my face, which had become popular/notorious in recent months. I was almost halfway through my cigarette when they decided to attack me from all sides. They rushed out of the darkness with urban battle cries. The fuckers didn't bother with threats or posturing. Their silly hope was that their numbers would throw me off just long enough for one of them to put me down.

Under the light, I should've been a fragile human. As I hopped off the picnic table and looked up at the streetlight, I felt anything but fragile. The nearest junkie took an open-palm to the sternum. His corpse flew off into the bushes. I ducked under a thrown beer bottle, caught it, and then backhanded it across the once-pretty face of a waifish young woman. Dazed, she dropped her blade, which I caught. I then used her as a human shield as one of them emptied a .22 into her. I dropped her scrawny corpse. Then my underhanded throw sank her knife into the shooter's throat.

Two of them turned and sprinted away, leaving three behind. A fat motherfucker rushed in and tried a rear bear hug. I spun and grabbed his throat with both hands. Easily 6'4", he tried to pull free of my 5'8" death grip . . . until I crushed his neck. Another junkie opted to flee, leaving just one more.

The only super in the bunch, I gazed over his one power—one the junkie probably didn't even know he had. If he did, the natural-born super wouldn't have been wasting his time mugging people. With the right training, he could've been a world-class thief.

His body generated a natural bio-field which (in effect) made him invisible to most tech. Motion sensors? HD security cameras? Voice recognition software? Nada. Since the power was constantly active, the smelly fuck would have to consciously turn it off to be scanned. Had we met under different circumstances, I could've turned him into a high-end asset.

What a waste.

Caught in the throes of withdrawal, the terrified twenty-something shivered as I slowly approached him. In his grimy hands was a graffiti-covered baseball bat. Even with the shakes, his tiny mind was weighing the odds of killing me with it.

My left hand pulled the wakizashi from its sheath. His eyes widened with fear as he made his choice and swung on me. I sidestepped his desperate lunge and sliced through his wooden bat like it was a giant loaf of French bread. The shocked super was left with only a handle. He eyed me over his left shoulder just as I stabbed him through it.

He shrieked through rotting teeth. The bat's handle fell from his fingers as I grabbed his neck and ripped him. Five months ago, I could've fed on his mind and/or life energy. Neither power worked now. As he dropped to his knees and wailed, the super was too busy bleeding to do much else than suffer.

I tried a power rip and . . . it worked!

A slow smile crossed my face as I withdrew the blade and left the fucker to bleed out. I felt whole again. For two decades, whether I was running black ops or discreetly using it as a fixer, the ability defined me. My power rips used to be temporary. I knew how to use the borrowed abilities as well as their rightful owners—sometimes better. I could even turn them on and off whenever I chose.

Back when my augmentations were new, I could steal dozens of super powers for over a week at a time. On the night I died, I could barely keep a handful of them for longer than a few minutes. Curious about my current limits, I turned off the sensor stealth power. I needed to be bait right now. Besides, if Grace lost track of me, my ArgoKnight "allies" might overreact.

I took off my right glove and used the power gaze on myself. This was getting better and better! My regenerative powers were back, which must've been Band-Aid's intention. The feisty ability was relentless enough to (hopefully) destroy the chemical leash and keep me alive.

Band-Aid had managed to merge my old augmentation with my shadow mutation. How, I had no idea (but I was gonna find out). My physical abilities were at full capacity, whether in the presence of light or not. The shadowportation was back at full (global) range. Relieved, I unfastened the damaged flight collar and slipped it into my coat.

Unfortunately, I couldn't control shadows anymore. It also looked like my powers were . . . "darkness-dependent." I could actually store darkness somehow, like a solar-powered device stored light. Once the "charge" ran out, I'd be human again. If stuck under bright light for too long, my powers would all cut off.

That's all my power gaze would tell me. Band-Aid would have to fill in the blanks. Right now, I had to get my mask and goggles back. Then I'd stop Connor from wiping out my fucking city.

CHAPTER TEN

I fell out of the shadows and found myself alone at the damaged work site. The place was just as empty (and wrecked) as we left it. With this much structural damage, I wondered if Gratte would bother finishing the lair or not. I put on my mask on and then the sensor goggles. Curious, I scanned the building for any other surprises.

Most of his team's abandoned equipment and tools were intact. No casualties, which was a good thing. The psychic radiation was already dissipating. The goggles estimated that it would be completely gone in about six hours.

In the distance, I could hear sirens. I wasn't surprised that someone called the police. What bothered me was that the fucking cops had actually chosen to show up. Such a prompt response usually meant that someone with power had made that phone call.

I tapped my wristcom.

"Grace, what's our status?"

"Gratte's perimeter sensors are erased, as of four minutes ago," she replied. "I see that the cops are here in record time."

I could tell that the former detective was just as intrigued as I was. After all, Pillar City cops hated superhuman crime calls. Their slow response time (at least thirty minutes) was a courtesy to the perps involved. It gave the super crooks time to finish their crimes and get away clean. Then the police would come along and foul up the investigation . . . for a fee.

Of course, if you didn't pay up, they would find you. Worse, they'd arrest you at your worst possible moment. Even I was paying bribes—but not to them. I donated campaign money to the mayor, the D.A., and every judge in town. With that level of protection, the precincts couldn't arrest me—another reason they wanted me so very dead.

"Who sent them?" Grace wondered. "The O'Flernans?"

Thinking back to Glue's high-speed pursuit and the shootout at *Smitty's*, I wouldn't be surprised.

"Find out," I told her.

"Copy that," she replied. "Anything else?"

"Yeah. Gratte's gear's all over the place. Have Anywhere scoop it up."

"The scene'll be crawling with cops in ten seconds," Grace complained. "He won't have enough time."

"I'll buy him some," I grinned as I ran toward a large shadow and created a tunnel from it.

"Cly, don't do anything stupid—" Grace managed to say before I shadowported.

"*Moi*?!" I laughed as I burst out from under Connor's beat-up Lexus and flipped it over.

Moving way too fast at the time, the stolen car went flying. Sparks flew as it landed upside-down and skimmed asphalt for half a block. As luck would have it, traffic was light on this street.

"I thought you couldn't shadowport past 80 yards," Grace worriedly remarked.

"So did I," I lied as I spotted a nearby Taco Bell. "Must be the fresh air."

Connor climbed out of the wrecked car. He looked my way and shook his head with amazement. Then his expression darkened, promising me a large amount of painful violence. Unfortunately for him the asshole was standing in the wrecked car's shadow. The entity comically yelped as the ground disappeared from beneath his feet and he fell into shadow.

"Where'd you send him?" Grace asked.

"Jove Street," I replied, happy that my goggles were recording all of this. "I've gotta go, Grace. Evil's afoot."

"You can't just send him there!" she scolded me.

"Why not?" I asked through a giggle.

Sounds of screams and gunfire emerged from the other end.

"Oh, right!" I said with fake surprise. "The cops."

"Cly—"

"Don't worry, Grace," I falsely assured her, "the police are trained for this sort of thing. Everything'll be just fine."

My stomach grumbled with sudden hunger. Pleased that my cravings were still food-based, I headed for Taco Bell and waited in line. Then I ordered ten soft tacos and two large Mountain Dews. The cashier loved my "Cly costume" and asked me where I got it. Amused, I paid for my meal and left.

I stepped around the building and formed a shadow tunnel. Aiming it at Gratte, I was curious to see whether or not he was alone. I peered through it to find Gratte standing on the rooftop of a four-story apartment building. Judging from the gunfire, he wasn't too far from where I sent Connor.

In spite of his stressful lifestyle, Gratte looked to be a decade younger than his fifty-one years. He was one of the few people on God's Earth I'd ever let myself trust. He stood a few inches taller than me, wearing beige cargo pants and a white golf shirt over his mild gut. Gratte's tan was always a bit much, like he wanted everyone to think he was Italian. A gray *Lairs 'R Us* cap was pulled down over his neat mane of black-dyed hair. With a friendly face that clashed with his obnoxious demeanor, Gratte had that "pal-of-mine" charisma and a loyalty that was utterly canine.

Too bad he was also an asshole. Just ask any of his four ex-wives.

Certain that he was alone, I shadowported to his location. Instead of a shadow tunnel, I created a portal. They took more effort but were useful—especially when carrying drinks. Instead of falling through shadow, I merely stepped through it like a doorway. On the other side, Gratte watched the noisy violence below with a disapproving sigh. I turned off my goggles, wristcom, and then kicked on the sensor stealth power.

"Talk freely," I said, as I pulled my mask up to my nose. "Grace can't eavesdrop on us right now."

"You're a real asshole. Y'know that?" Gratte griped.

The gruff-voiced bastard had a thick New York accent and no qualms about profanity or slutty women.

"I learned from the best," I replied. "Hungry?"

Gratte eyed my face for a moment and then snatched a Mountain Dew from my right hand. Then I handed him a straw and sat down. I wasn't close enough to the roof's edge to see the carnage but I could hear it just fine.

"I take it you were briefed on tonight's events?" I asked as I set my bags down on the rooftop and put a straw in my cup.

Gratte didn't reply for a few seconds, probably wondering if I was here to kill him.

"You're fucking up a perfectly good arrangement," he argued. "How far would you have gotten without the ArgoKnights' help?"

"We needed each other," I countered. "But, don't forget that you idiots *fucking poisoned me*."

"What?" he frowned.

"Don't play dumb with me, Gratte!" I seethed.

Gratte took a thoughtful swig of Mountain Dew.

"It wasn't my idea," he conceded. "Band-Aid says your DNA's stable, by the way. Congratulations."

"Please keep that little secret between us," I told him.

Gratte sullenly nodded as I tossed him a taco. He began to unwrap it.

"You still should've told me," I sulked.

"You'd have gone apeshit, Cly," Gratte argued. "Before the therapy, you were getting downright scary. If you lost control and went full psi-vamp, you'd have been feeding on people right-and-left. The chemical leash was an insurance policy."

"Why didn't you have Band-Aid cure me back then?"

"We tried," Gratte replied through a mouthful of taco. "She couldn't."

I looked up at the (real) night sky and sighed.

"Did Grace know?"

"She was the only one who opposed the idea," Gratte muttered. "Grace figured that you'd kill us— whether you lost control or not."

She was right.

I unwrapped a taco and bit into it, bothered by the fact that Gratte was still a fucking ArgoKnight. Trained to be a Support Staff operative, he was put in charge of Pillar City's intelligence ops just after 9/11. We both came to the city that year. He pretended to be freelance muscle, trying to earn the trust (and secrets) of the city's underworld. I was a new fixer, out to make a fortune off the War On Terror.

Gratte was one of my first contractors. The human had a gift for gab and crime, with leadership chops worth his weight in gold. So, when I came up with the *Lairs 'R Us* scheme, I put him in charge of it. The whole thing worked like a charm . . . until Grace fucked up his cover.

Last October, Grace needed to find a decommissioned 80's-era Way Station in Uptown. Thing was, she didn't know where it was. The only reason I knew was that Gratte had purchased the house it was built under. When he found out that said house came with a lair, Gratte called me. Grace eavesdropped on the call and asked me for the address, citing a need to save the city. I took her to the site, where we needed an impossibly rare piece of ArgoKnight tech to bring the place on-line. Guess who left one lying around his equipment site?

Leo Gratte.

Had Grace known that Gratte was Support Staff, she'd have gone directly to him. Instead, I got involved. We used the Way Station's resources to save two million lives and ultimately 99% of everyone else's too. After that fucked-up night, I realized that Gratte's discovery of the lair wasn't an "accident." Gratte wanted me to find it.

To this day, he never told me why.

Once I put two-and-two together, I went after him. The bastard didn't hide, fight, or beg. Instead of drinking his memories or shooting him dead, I spared his sorry ass. My reasons were simple enough.

Lairs 'R Us hadn't been confiscated by the mobs (like my other assets). Killing him would be bad for business. Add to that the ArgoKnights (and his own staff) might choose to come after me. Besides, his actions had helped save the city and my kid.

Sparing him made us even.

Ever since then, I figured that we had an understanding. He'd work for me and the ArgoKnights without betraying the loyalty of either. This too might've worked had his pals not decided to poison me. Now, Gratte would have to pick a side. Judging from his tone, it wouldn't be mine.

"Connor's pretty pissed off," Gratte said between mouthfuls, his eyes on the slaughter below.

"Imagine being stuck in someone else's head for a decade," I muttered, looking up at the moon. "Wouldn't you be?"

I laid back on the rooftop, ate tacos, and brushed crumbs off my costume. More shooting and crunching sounds echoed through the night. A uniformed cop was sent screaming past the rooftop and out of sight. What followed was a gooey-sounding impact, which made me smile.

"You're gonna let this go on?!" Gratte asked, trying to appeal to my sense of guilt.

"Better them than me," I muttered. "And Leo, don't the cops have unofficial orders to shoot me on sight?"

Gratte paused with a calculating frown as I tossed him a second taco.

"They can't stop him, Cly."

"True," I agreed. "But they can make him burn through his reserves. Then Connor dies and the world's a better place."

Then again, there was another factor in play. If Connor died, his son would die soon after. That was the bitch about two-way psychic links as old as theirs. I don't think Gratte figured that part out yet.

"That's your plan? Burn him out?" Gratte asked.

"Duh," I replied as I bit into my fifth taco. "Besides, this gives Anywhere enough time to save your expensive equipment. No need to thank me."

Gratte unwrapped his taco and sipped his soda. There was another explosion. Some more screams and the sounds of a car being used as a sledgehammer. Gratte finished his taco and set his drink down. Then he fished a pack of slim cigars from his pants and pulled one out with a sad smile.

"It's a shame," Gratte muttered as he put the pack away. "In an alternate reality, you could've been an ArgoKnight. Maybe the best of us all."

"Nah," I shook my head. "Besides this reality's a lot more fun."

The sounds of incoming choppers could be heard. We both looked up as a pair of black SWAP helicopters swooped in. While SWAT meant Special Weapons and Tactics, SWAP meant Special Weapons and Powers. Every big city had (at least) one. The closest thing to a super team, they handled the big bad threats to the city— when possible, anyway. Our local SWAP cops only came out for press briefings, documentaries, and PR gigs.

They've also been known to moonlight as freelance killers.

"I thought our SWAP team was a myth," Gratte joked. "When was the last time these bozos handled a real case?"

I frowned with contemplation.

"That giant frog monster thing," I recalled. "That was '06, right?"

"'07," Gratte corrected me.

Eight super cops fast-roped toward the street below. They wore black and were kitted out like a human SWAT team, only with better weaponry. Before they descended below my line of sight, I gazed them over. Most of them were supers with decent powers. I couldn't read three of them, which meant they were cyborgs. They didn't let "token" humans join because they always died.

After *Clean Sweep,* most of the would-be super heroes ended up wearing badges instead. Those few who were chosen to be SWAP cops tended to ex-super soldiers, back from either Afghanistan or a post-nuclear

Iran. Both wars left a lot of ex-vets looking for better pay and some high-order action.

While it was a lot safer than being a hero, their ability to do good was limited by red tape and the lack of anonymity. The most effective super cops (whether detectives or SWAP) usually ended up dead, on the take, or cowed into submission by threats to their families.

Right now, I had the nagging suspicion that Pillar City's SWAP team was about to die. Both choppers had a human door gunner and a mounted .50-cal machine gun. They cut loose with tracer rounds.

"Amateurs!" Gratte muttered as he flicked open his lighter. "Bullets against an energy form never work."

Two of the SWAP members were telepaths. If they combined their attacks, they might give Connor a fight. If that didn't work, they shouldn't stand a chance.

"Another taco?" I offered.

"No thanks," he replied. "Lia kicked some ass tonight."

"Saw the footage, eh?" I grinned.

"Yeah," Gratte smiled. "You trained her well."

Actually, I paid other people to train her but I accepted the praise anyway. Eyes on the carnage, Gratte simply shook his head. The choppers moved in closer (which was fucking stupid). Something else exploded. There was more shooting and some flashes of energy as the super cops cut loose.

"Overpaid idiots!" Gratte snorted through a plume of cigar smoke. "My underwear could fight better than these pricks."

As if to make his point, a screaming SWAP cop was hurled *through* one of the choppers. It exploded. As the burning mass of metal dropped toward the street, the screaming super continued off into the night.

"C'mon Cly! Get in there!" Gratte yelled, unable to endure the sight of such a one-sided ass kicking.

"Fuck!" I sighed as I tapped my wristcom. "Anywhere, what's your status?"

"Just about done," came his reply.

"Y'know Gratte," I said as I stood up and walked past him. "In an alternate reality, I wouldn't be an ArgoKnight. I'd be killing your pals . . . and maybe you too. You know why?"

"No. Why?"

"Evil's more fun," I replied. "Always will be."

Gratte gave me the finger as I grabbed my soda, created a new shadow tunnel, and then dove into it. I fell out of a crushed police cruiser's shadow and surveyed the scene. The fight was almost over.

A trio of super-strong SWAP cops had managed to wrestle Connor to the street. I looked around for the telepaths. One of them was missing his head. The other one lay dying. A piece of shrapnel had gone through her left leg. Judging from the pooling blood, it nicked her artery.

Unconscious and pale, the telepath was kinda cute. With my right boot, I nudged her toward a convenient-sized shadow. As I created the tunnel, I aimed the poor piggy toward the St. George's ER section. Assuming the trip didn't kill her, they might be able to save her. Anyone seeing this would've thought I was saving her life.

In reality, I just wanted her powers.

My boot tap took her modest-level telepathy, telekinesis, and (oh!) memory editing. These'll come in handy. As the shadow portal closed, I casually sipped my drink and took in the mayhem. The remaining chopper had to hold fire while the three supers tried to clamp a blue inhibitor collar around Connor's neck.

I enjoyed my caffeinated beverage and waited for the cops to die. Their problem was inadequate gear. Inhibitor collars generated a steady, short-ranged energy pulse that could negate most superhuman abilities. The problem was that they were meant to be used on flesh-and-blood types. Besides, from this range, it looked like a Mark-5 collar. Even cut off from the psi-link, Connor's energy form might be too powerful.

They clamped the collar on him and foolishly relaxed their grip, thinking him contained. Connor got an arm loose and punched a SWAP cop right through his torso. Gross . . . yet efficient. The other two cops tried (and failed) to muscle him down again. The second cop got his throat ripped open. The entity hurled the last one through the second police chopper, right as the door gunner opened fire again.

I laughed at the explosion and subsequent crash. Then I took a last sip of Mountain Dew and tossed the cup. With all of this debris, who'd care? Covered in cop blood, the psychic entity noticed me as I stepped forward and pulled my mask back down. Now that I was more evolved, I felt oh-so ready for round two.

CHAPTER ELEVEN

"You should be in the next *Spider-Man* flick," I told Connor as I approached. "If you need an agent, I could make a few calls."

"Where's my son, you freak?!" he roared.

"Hopefully on a mortician's slab," I taunted as I power gazed him. "I warned you that it would end in tears, didn't I?"

Guess that SWAP collar wasn't so useless after all. The big guy was getting weaker by the second. Either Connor realized that he was fucked or he was more worried about his son. Honestly, I didn't care. With both of them dead, the world was a safer place—simple as that. As Connor strode toward me, I cut off my sensor stealth.

"I'll just have to tear the truth out of you then," Connor said with a hateful smile.

The O'Flernan rushed in and swung at me with everything he had left. I easily blocked the right roundhouse as my hands found the front of his suit jacket. Even though it was made of pure energy, it felt like the real thing. With a snarl, I twisted Connor over my right shoulder and flung him through a parked police cruiser.

The Irish bastard unsteadily rose to his feet, more bothered by his dying mind than by any physical injury. After Connor climbed out of the wrecked vehicle, he paused and tried to rip the collar off. After several seconds, he gave up.

With both hands, I beckoned him to come at me again. Connor defiantly rushed in to tackle my legs. I easily sidestepped his clumsy effort and tripped his right leg out from under him. Down he went. I folded my arms and shook my head with pure mockery.

A white Channel 4 news chopper flew overhead. It shined a spotlight down on us as Connor slowly (almost achingly) rose to his feet. My goggles instantly tinted to compensate.

"I'm gonna . . . gonna kill you!" Connor growled, as his energy form began to dissipate. "You and Ronns both!"

"Ronns?" I frowned.

Above me, the news chopper threw up plenty of noise and wind.

"What's your beef with Ronns?" I shouted as Connor tried in vain to stand up. "Tell it true and your kid might not end up in a shallow grave."

Connor glared up at me and saw that I wasn't bluffing. He quit trying to move.

"Ronns killed me and my brother," he conceded.

Connor wasn't lying.

That didn't mean that I believed it, though. Harlan Ronns was a sadist, a killer, and a loyal foot soldier for the O'Flernan mob. One could argue that he killed Angus and Connor as some kind of power play with the goal of taking over. As a Shepherd, the fucker was Seamus' right-hand man. For any other mob, such a thing wasn't too far-fetched.

The thing was a Shepherd's role came with a glass ceiling of sorts. Only hard-core sadists were picked to be Shepherds (like Ronns). Accepting the mantle meant that they could never run the mob. It was an unspoken rule in the O'Flernan mob. Their sins were always too many (and too sickening) to inspire loyalty among the underbosses.

"Bullshit," I told him. "Ronns was your dad's Shepherd for almost fifteen years. He'd eat a bullet for either one of you."

"It was Ronns," Connor replied with hateful certainty. "He set off the bomb himself!"

Ronns would only kill the O'Flernan brothers with Seamus' say-so; something the old man would never do. He was always worried about his legacy. Killing both of his criminal heirs made no sense.

"Please!" Connor pleaded, "Please spare my son. Please—"

That's when Connor passed out and began to fade away. I should just let death take its course. The thing was I had to know if Connor was completely honest. Besides, the unconscious entity was well past harmless.

I kicked on the cop's telepathy, slipped in, and grabbed a quick peek . . .

Damn this setting sun. Should've brought my sunglasses.

"I'm tellin' you," Angus grinned as he locked the door, "you aren't getting into Debbie's skirt."

"There's no pair of legs I can't navigate," I replied as I turned the key. "It'll take just a bit more time is all."

Angus' GTO purred like always. I'd let him drive his own car but we were running late and had no time for traffic laws.

I started to back out of the garage when Angus' phone rang. Probably Vivian again. They'd been having a lot of "meetings" lately—something about an overseas land deal. With legs like Hallett's, I might've fit her into my schedule too. Faced with Da's pressure to settle down, my kid brother might've been interested in something serious.

A tigress between the sheets, Vivian was way too smart to be that fine. Worse, she was a lawyer. I'd have to keep an eye on her.

"Hi Viv," Angus smiled as I turned us around. "Yes, they know to let you into the sky box."

He glanced at his watch, then over at me.

"The way Connor drives? We'll get there yesterday."

If the driveway didn't have a blind curve, I'd floor it right now. Instead, I gave Angus a nodding grin and rolled us past the house. Along the way, I caught a glimpse of Ronns. Standing in the kitchen window, he waved farewell with his right hand. In his left was a little black box, which he pointed in our direction.

There was a sudden beeping sound under my seat—

What followed next was an abrupt pain and then blackness.

My mild, telepathic contact with Connor was like giving air to a drowning man. His energy form stopped fading out. I felt his mind instinctively claw at mine, trying to establish a stable psi-link. Well, fuck that. Once I broke my psi-link with Connor, he'd die (for good) in a matter of seconds. The kid would die soon after but that might've been for the best—

I screamed as my goggles strobe-flashed right in my fucking eyes!

The sharp, disorienting agony flat-out blinded me. I ripped the goggles off and staggered away from Connor, utterly vulnerable. It was an ambush. Connor's mind screamed too, equally fucked up by my pain. Such was the downside of a psi-link.

I dropped to a knee and quickly locked the entity away within a deep hole in my mind—just in case I needed more answers from him later. My eyes were healing up but not fast enough. Fists clenched, I stood up and waited for the rest of the ambush. The damned chopper made it impossible to smell or hear shit—

That's when I got sucker-punched.

Someone popped me right in the face, harder than I've ever been hit in my entire goddamned life. I smashed straight through a bunch of buildings, a tree (maybe?), and some more buildings. Eventually, a very thick wall brought me to a painful stop.

I slid to the floor, surprised to be alive. My mouth was filled with blood. I had a broken nose, jaw, both shoulders, some ribs, and a few missing teeth by my rough estimate. Barely conscious, I couldn't feel my legs. Spinal damage, I imagined. Without my costume, that blow would've outright killed me.

Only the shock kept me conscious.

My goggles had strobe-flashed me from the inside. Seeing as Gunrack had personally designed them for me, I was being attacked by ArgoKnights.

Luckily, my body was still able to regenerate. Broken bones and torn muscles painfully began to snap back into their normal locations. Still, whoever put me down wouldn't have just left me here. I was at the mercy of my attacker(s), which meant that they'd show up to finish me off.

My ears healed up just in time to hear hover thrusters. I smiled as I recognized that sound. It was Lia; my little armored Valkyrie. Still on overwatch, Grace must've sent my kid in to back me up. I felt my eyes open and realized that I was in the shattered lobby of a post office. Through my mask, I could see her fly over a damaged building and land at the shattered entrance. I had to warn her about the ArgoKnights before they got her too.

"Lia!" I gasped, still unable to move. "It's a setup! We need to get out of here!"

"I'm sorry, Dad," Lia replied as she cautiously advanced.

That's when I saw blood on her right fist . . .

Time seemed to stop. It was Lia—she hit me! That wasn't possible. There had to be someone else in that armor! Even though Samir had built a dozen fail-safes against such a possibility, it was the only thing that made sense. There was no way she would've (could've) done this!

"Just lie still," she urged me with a soothing tone. "Your DNA's regressing. My sensors have you regenerating; just like when you were drinking minds."

Oh fuck! Lia was scared of me during that dark time. She saw the hunger in my eyes, back before I asked ACHE for help. I slowly shook my head as the inhibitor needle slid out of her left palm. The SWAP cop's memory editing abilities came to mind. The problem was that her armor came with psi-shielding. Between that and her still-formidable will, I'd have to go with the telekinesis.

"I'm eight different types of injured," I croaked. "Cut my powers and I'm dead."

"We have a team of healers on standby," she assured me. "You'll be fine."

Lia leaned over to dose me. I kicked on the telekinesis and sent her flying. The effort of that one attack felt like an ice pick shoved through my skull. The kid slammed into a nearby wall of P.O. boxes and rolled into a low crouch. Without the armor, I would've knocked her out. Instead, Lia quickly rose to her feet, ready to throw down.

"Think, Lia!" I croaked. "Look at my blood. It's red. Not black!"

"You're a threat, Dad!" she stubbornly replied. "We have to stop the regression before it becomes permanent!"

Anywhere teleported Pinpoint onto the scene.

They looked different.

While Anywhere still had his odd black costume on, the shotgun was gone. In his hands was a compact kinetic blaster. He held it expertly, without the usual incompetence I had come to expect from the teleporter. My aching eyes also noticed his new belt badge. It had a white knight logo on it, surrounded by a single word: ArgoKnights.

Pinpoint wore a matching badge.

This wasn't happening!

From the neck-down, my one-time ace shooter wore a curve-hugging suit of crimson body armor. Attached to that armor were an ArgoKnight-issue utility harness and five holstered sidearms (hips, shoulders, and right ankle). In Pinpoint's hands was a nasty-looking carbine with an under-barrel energy weapon of some kind.

At twenty-nine, the freckled killer was tall and slim. Her cute face was oddly amused as a breeze blew in and caught her brown ponytail. Like Anywhere, she sported sensor goggles. In her left ear was a small metallic earpiece.

"Target contained," Pinpoint reported. "Rounding him up now."

"ArgoKnights?!" I laughed/coughed. "You two are ArgoKnights?!"

Anywhere was a putz. Pinpoint's kill count was in the low thousands. Maybe they were Support Staff, which allowed for undercover operatives. That followed. Still, per the old rules, ArgoKnight Support Staffers couldn't wear the logo. It was a status reserved for the heroes.

I guess they got promoted.

"Told you he had no idea," Anywhere smirked through his balaclava. He glanced over at Lia. "You okay?"

"Careful," Lia warned them, "he can rip powers again."

The two ArgoKnights raised their guns. While Anywhere might be a concern, I was more worried about Pinpoint. If it came with a trigger, she couldn't miss—that was her power. I was also certain that Pinpoint's weaponry would punch through my costume just fine.

As full-on ArgoKnights, they were now bound by a Code of Conduct that limited their actions in a variety of situations. Pinpoint couldn't (technically) kill anyone ever again. If she got caught, the rules called for her to be kicked off the team and incarcerated.

"We should dose him now," Lia warned.

I winced as I felt sudden pain in my legs. Pain was good. I needed to buy some time.

"Wait," I chuckled. "Lemme get this straight; Anywhere's not some limp-dicked waste of manhood?"

"Ding!" Anywhere sarcastically replied. "Just a cover."

Lia moved between them with that exposed needle still in her palm.

"What now?" I asked. "You dose me, put on another chemical leash, and then send me home?"

"Oh no, Cly," Pinpoint smiled. "Once we neuter your powers, you're going into a well-lit stasis cell for the rest of your life."

I looked up at Lia, who shook her head.

"It's only temporary," she lamely countered.

Sadly, my kid didn't have the final say in my fate.

"You could wipe my memories," I offered. "Do it right and I'll never know what kind of back-stabbing cunts you really are."

Anywhere looked over at Pinpoint.

"I'm really gonna miss his gift for gab," he mocked.

"And I'm gonna miss laughin' at you," I replied. "You're such a little bitch that my kid—without her fucking armor—is more dangerous than you."

Anywhere glared daggers at me. Even though I was able to move, I faked a cough and played helpless as I looked over at Pinpoint.

"You two were Support Staff spies this whole time?"

The shooter nodded without a hint of regret.

"We tracked most of your fixer ops," Pinpoint gloated. "After *Clean Sweep*, you even did a few jobs for us."

I gave them a weak shrug. Back in the day, I arranged jobs for so many anonymous clients that I wouldn't have been surprised. As long as the checks cleared, I was cool.

"Just stay still, Dad," Lia said as she inched a bit closer. "Once we get you back to base, we'll cure this regression and everything'll be fine."

"They're here to kill me, kid," I told her. "If they wanted me alive, they'd have shown up with non-lethal ordinance."

Lia turned and eyed her colleagues' weapons.

"They must've lost friends because of me," I stalled. "Am I right?"

Pinpoint's face reddened.

"Your mom?" I asked. "Did I have your mommy killed, Pinpoint? Your daddy, perhaps? There were so many—"

"It was my sister, asshole!" Pinpoint snapped.

"Ah. Who was she?" I asked, genuinely curious.

"Quiver," she replied.

I couldn't see the resemblance but I remembered the name. Quiver was a master archer who used trick arrows and telekinesis in her fight against evil. During *Clean Sweep,* one of my teams captured her. So many villains wanted to buy captured heroes back then that I got in on the action. While I forgot who I sold

Pinpoint's sister to, I'm sure the poor gal's dead and gone by now.

"What about you?" I asked Anywhere. "Who'd you lose?"

"Impasse was my mentor," Anywhere angrily added.

"Really?" I nodded, remembering the masked hero. "Now *he* was worth big money. Died well, too. Took four of my best with him. Sorry he couldn't 'man' you up first."

Anywhere's grip tightened on his weapon.

"Stop provoking them," Lia cut in, as she waved her colleagues back. "Stick to the plan, guys."

Anywhere and Pinpoint reluctantly nodded.

"I'm not trusting these motherfuckers," I told her.

"Your mutation can't be contained anymore," Lia explained, not realizing that Band-Aid was the reason for my resurgence. "It's only gonna get worse. We're just going to quarantine you until we find a cure."

It was a stalemate.

If Lia came any closer, there'd be a fight. Not only was I regenerating, I had telekinesis, which she wisely kept between us. The kid knew that I couldn't hurt her but I could hurt Pinpoint and Anywhere. Frankly, I should've snapped their necks a few minutes ago. Still, if they died, Lia could easily kick my ass (again) with that armor.

"You don't get it, kid," I growled. "My powers are stable, which has them scared. Without their chemical leash, I'm harder to kill, especially with my old augmentations added in."

"How do you know that your mutation's stable?" Lia argued. "That you won't turn?"

"Simple," I sighed. "If I turned, you'd all be snacks by now."

I couldn't see her face but I knew Lia was scared shitless. Turned or not, I wasn't going down without a fight. Anywhere and Pinpoint thought they had the upper hand as they impatiently waited for the signal to attack.

"Besides," I added, "you expect me to trust these fuckers?! *They poisoned me.*"

I expected that last part to shock her. Instead, Lia shook her armored head.

"No, Dad. I poisoned you."

CHAPTER TWELVE

The chopper's spotlight shined into the lobby. The back draft from the rotors whipped around us. For a moment, all I could do was gawk at my daughter.

"You hear that?" Anywhere said with a hateful smile. "That's the sound of Cly's soul breaking."

I slowly stood up.

Pinpoint's eyes were locked on mine. I knew that the moment I made a wrong move the bitch would "accidentally" put a bullet right through my skull. Anywhere looked equally ready to open fire. I wondered if the "non-killing" section of the ArgoKnight rulebook had been discarded altogether.

Well, so much for talking . . .

The standard ArgoKnight utility sash (like the one Pinpoint was wearing) had its gadgets set in a pre-arranged order. That way, if one of her teammates needed to pull a gadget from it, they could do so without delay or confusion.

I counted down to the fifth pouch and reached out with the telekinesis. I (hopefully) squeezed one of the three marble grenades on her utility sash. Named for its shape, the red explosive had twice the bang of an Embedder round. The five-second countdown began. The sensors in Lia's armor should warn her riiight about . . .

"Dad, I'll explain it all later," Lia said as she stepped in to dose me. "First, we need to get you–"

Her head whipped toward Pinpoint's utility sash.

"Don't move!" my kid yelled as she rushed toward Pinpoint.

Lia clamped both hands around the gadget's pouch. A half-second later, there was a muffled *BOOM* between her armor's gauntlets as the tiny explosive went off.

Pinpoint winced as Lia's gauntlets completely absorbed the explosive energy—just like Samir had designed them.

I dove at Anywhere who turned his rifle my way and squeezed the trigger. Right before he could fire, I telekinetically pointed his gun at Lia's back. The bluish kinetic blast slammed into her armor and sent both ladies flying. Lia should be okay.

Pinpoint . . . I really didn't care anymore.

I punched Anywhere across the face. Since I couldn't rip powers from dead supers, I pulled my strike (this time). Anywhere hit the floor and nimbly rolled to one knee. Blood began to pour from his nose as he blinked in surprise. I gave him a smug middle finger.

"Hey! Gimme back my power!" Anywhere yelled as he raised his weapon to fire again.

By then, Lia and I were gone in an implosion of air.

Grace Lexia was hunched over her laptop when Lia stumbled past her. Her armored hands were still smoking from the marble bomb. The psi-hacker could only gawk up at me as I plopped down in one of her two guest chairs. Anywhere's power had brought us to a small, windowless office. It came with white walls, gray carpeting, and all of the impersonal drabness of a not-so-new facility.

There was a large metal desk between Grace and myself. On it was her laptop and her large gray coffee mug. Behind her was that same brick wall I saw during our video chats. I didn't flinch as Grace pulled her Uzi out from under her desk. Terrified, she aimed the SMG at my masked face in a two-handed grip. Lia slipped into a fighting stance, ready to back Grace up if I stepped out of line.

With a sigh, I reached over and picked up the half-empty mug of lukewarm coffee from her desk. Then I wearily removed my mask and spat three bloody teeth into it. Their replacements were already growing inside my mouth. With a groan, I leaned back into the guest chair, mostly regenerated.

"So," I crossed my legs, "how many dead?"

Lia and Grace swapped glances as I slipped the mask into my coat pocket.

"What do you mean?" Lia asked.

"You knocked me through a bunch of buildings," I explained before giving Grace a withering glare. "Did anyone get killed in the process?"

Grace didn't lower her gun as she regarded her laptop. After a moment, the psi-hacker sighed and looked over at Lia with a disapproving frown.

"Fifteen injuries—two critical—reported in different buildings," Grace reported.

"You should've just dosed me," I told Lia. "I didn't see you coming."

"The Paucium might not have worked on you," Lia argued. "And before the gene therapy, you were shrugging off standard physical attacks. I couldn't hold back."

Lia could've nailed me with the tanglenets, grabbed me, and flew off. Hell, she could've just tried to talk me into coming in quietly. Lastly, her armor came with gobs of non-lethal shit capable of putting me down. It amazed me that she didn't use them.

"I hope you're not here for an apology," Grace dryly joked.

"No," I replied. "If it's not too much trouble, could you tell me why everyone's treating me like the Anti-Christ? Start with the part where I regress, 'cause I'm not feeling that."

Grace looked over at Lia and then carefully set the Uzi down next to the laptop (within easy reach). She slowly sat down and eyed me, internally debating on what to say.

"About a month after you died," Grace began, "we got intel that your mutation was unstable. Our estimates were that you'd become a feral killing machine within four months."

I quickly did the math.

"In other words . . . any day now?" I asked.

Grace nodded.

"I don't recall you mentioning this during our many briefings," I said.

"You were too busy hunting down the Black Wheel," Grace explained.

"In other words, my powers made me too 'useful' to cure?" I asked.

Grace nodded without a hint of shame. "While you were kicking ass, we were researching possible cures. Believe it or not, you weren't the only shadow mutation in our files."

"Any chance I could see these files?" I asked.

Grace shook her head.

"Anything resembling a cure?" I pressed.

"No," she replied. "We did find a formula for the chemical leash; one used by a crime lord to control his shadowpath."

The term brought a smile to my face.

"That's what you used on me?"

"Not at first," Grace explained. "Our original intent was to use the formula to reverse-engineer a cure."

She looked over at Lia.

"Unfortunately, you started losing control of your feeding impulses. When you came to us for help, we decided to use the leash."

"What about ACHE's gene therapy?" I asked. "That wouldn't have held?"

"On its own? No," Grace shook her head. "During the last round of therapy, your body began to adapt to—and reject—the process. Basically, Cly, your cells were *eating* the nanites."

Another fact they had neglected to mention.

"I see," I muttered with a frown at Lia. "That's when you decided to have my daughter poison me?"

"Would you have honestly let us dose you with a chemical leash, Cly?" Grace asked.

"If you gave me an informed choice? Yes."

"Why would you trust us?" Grace scoffed.

"Because I don't wanna turn into a rabid killing machine," I angrily replied. "Also, we were on the same side . . . until now."

I leaned forward.

"Lucky for me, I'm cured."

"No you're not," Lia cut in.

I sighed, bothered by her know-it-all attitude. Back when I was losing control of my "animal" side, I could feel it happening days in advance. If I were turning, I'd know it.

"What aren't you telling me?" I asked them.

Grace looked over at Lia and gave her a tense nod.

The armor slid open. Lia stepped out. She wasn't in her street clothing. Instead, she wore a gray-and-blue ArgoKnight uniform. The one-piece outfit was a bit thicker than a skin suit and probably armored, like my costume. The ArgoKnight logo was on the uniform's left torso. A team badge was on her belt just under her utility sash. They didn't give those to trainees. Only full-fledged members got them.

Lia had just made the dumbest mistake of her young life.

"When did they recruit you?" I asked with a disbelieving shake of my head.

"Five months ago," Lia replied as she folded her arms.

I set Grace's mug on her desk. "Explain yourself."

Lia nervously sighed.

"I thought I wanted to live your life. To be a fixer someday," she began. "I learned all of these cool things . . . so many things. I had this super power that could save lives and you let me use it."

Lia smiled.

"Then I saw you as a hero. Watched you save the world—*our world*. The world needs us, Dad. As many heroes as it can get. That's when I decided to become one, like you."

"Kid, I'm not a hero," I grinned. "I'm a crook who happens to fight crime."

Lia shrugged away my objection.

"Tell that to Juliette or the billions of lives you've saved."

My mind drifted to the scared little hooker that we saved.

"You'd never let me be a hero, Dad," Lia continued. "That's why I went to Grace and asked her to plug me in with the ArgoKnights."

"Why not strike out on your own?" I asked. "I'd have let you . . . when you were ready."

Lia gave me a skeptical frown at that last part. She knew I'd never let her be a hero, a merc, or anything else dangerous. I'd keep her safe 'til I was dead—and then some.

"Well, Dad, I'm ready now."

"Really?" I asked with a flicker of a smile.

Lia nodded. "And I'm not gonna quit."

The kid was stubborn, just like her mother.

"I thought you had to have super powers to be an ArgoKnight?"

The psi-hacker swallowed hard and then looked down at the carpet.

"I got my power back," she confessed. "Sort of."

Something in my facial reaction made her flinch. In all of the recent chaos, I hadn't gazed her.

Basically, Lia was supposed to be powerless. If anything, I might've checked her power to see how ruined it was. With a gaze, I could see that her precog was back—but different. It was like a broken vase that had been glued back together. While it was still a vase, it was glaringly imperfect. Still, her imperfect power had its interesting elements.

She wasn't really a precog anymore. Lia was more of an intuitive psychic.

The kid couldn't give people visions. They were hers alone. Also, she only seemed to have visions during moments of intense stress. Instead of seeing a specific target(s) in a specific future, her power would simply throw a random vision at her.

Stranger still, Lia could take a glance at someone and know their past, present, and future. Her mind would "scan" a target and feed her reliable psychic impressions. Whatever she wanted to know (strengths, weaknesses, or even favorite foods) would pop into her head as "hunches." With the right mindset, such a power could be downright lethal.

Lia had kept this from me—*from me*. Why? I had no fucking idea. I interlocked my fingers and fought to control my boiling rage.

"Teke cured you?"

"No," Lia shook her head. "My mind cured itself."

When it was intact, Lia's power actually sent someone else's mind into the future (for the briefest of moments). Also, she couldn't grant a person more than one vision per day. These psychic safeguards were now gone. Without them, the more she used her powers, the faster her precog would drive her mad.

"Shouldn't you be insane by now?"

"My ArgoKnight psi-screen protects me," Lia replied.

"Why didn't you tell me?" I asked with amazing restraint.

Lia was too ashamed to answer, so Grace cut in.

"We thought it would be safer if everyone thought that Lia's power was ruined," Grace explained with a hint of praise. "It's proven useful in more than one instance."

I looked Grace Lexia in the eye with dwindling restraint. The bitch had butted into my family life. Had this happened a year ago, I'd have killed a few of her closest relatives, just out of spite.

I took a deep, cleansing breath.

"What's your codename?"

"I stuck with Forecast," Lia timidly shrugged. "It felt right."

I nodded with a half-smile. "You'll make an excellent ArgoKnight."

Both ladies regarded me with mutual shock.

"What?" I chuckled. "You thought I was training her to be a crook?"

"The thought crossed our minds," Grace admitted.

"Then you're both equally stupid," I spat.

I fished out my Marlboros, only to end up with a flattened pack. I rolled my eyes and tossed it onto her desk. Then I pointed at Forecast.

"This kid was born under fire," I reminded Grace. "I left her to her grandparents, remember? She was supposed to live a happy, boring life."

I glared at Forecast.

"Then, I ended up raising you only because your precog abilities made you a target! I had my best train you. Shield you. Risk their fucking lives to keep you safe."

I let that sink in for a bit.

"I know fixers who'd have sold you, enslaved you, or used you as a genetic brood mare. Instead, I called you 'daughter' and trained you to survive. You know why?"

Forecast shook her head.

"Me neither," I replied with pure venom. "Now get the fuck out of my sight!"

Forecast took a half-step back. I had never sworn at my daughter before. She saw my candid fury for the first time and it frightened her. Tears formed in her eyes.

"Dad—"

"Don't call me that again," I coldly interrupted. "Never again."

Out of the corner of my eye, Grace eyed the Uzi and licked her dry lips.

"You wanna sneak around and play hero? Fine," I ruefully smiled. "You wanna judge me, poison me, and use me as a goddamned lab rat? Fine. Betray my trust and damn-near kill me? Such is life."

I rose with an ominous slowness.

"What you do not get to do is called me 'Dad.' You've lost that right."

I glanced at Forecast's armor and thought of Jason Mallorix, the first guy I ever killed. While he was ninety-eight years old, the super's only power was longevity. He didn't look a day over thirty when I shot him in the head and left him to die in a gutter. The shock on his face was so pronounced that I could never forget it.

"Self-destruct code: Mallorix-98-Gutter."

The verbal command caused Samir's two billion-dollar armor to harmlessly collapse. Forecast's jaw dropped with loss and horror as the armor self-corroded into a pile of worthless junk. Within seconds, it was beyond salvage.

It was a failsafe (one of many). One I never thought I'd use.

"What did you do?!" Forecast gasped.

"As of right now, you're nothing to me," I told her. "Your things will be left outside. Enter my building again and you'll be treated as a hostile."

I turned toward Grace.

"Please tell Gunrack to immediately leave town."

That caught the psi-hacker by surprise.

"Cly—" Grace started to say.

"You heard me."

"She doesn't answer to you," Grace said with surprising, stupid defiance. "If you mess with her, the rest of us will come down on your head."

I gave her a steely grin. Then I casually (one-handedly) flung Grace's desk away from Forecast. Both of them gawked as the heavy piece of furniture slammed against the wall. Grace's Uzi fell to the floor, next to her shattered laptop. The psi-hacker backed up against the brick wall, wondering if I'd kill her.

To be honest, I hadn't yet made up my mind.

"Maybe I fucking stuttered," I replied as I quietly got into Grace's face. "If Gunrack's still in my area code in 24 hours, I will kill her and not think twice about it."

I glanced at a wall clock and saw that it was almost 1 a.m.

"Her clock starts now," I told her. "Pass the word."

I pulled out Gunrack's special guns. Surprised that they were crushed too, I handed them to Grace barrel-down. The psi-hacker's hands visibly shook as she

accepted them. I ripped the wristcom off my arm and
dropped it with a hateful grin.

"You know what's funny?" I chuckled. "You idiots
think you're better than me. I may have done a ton of
horrible things, Grace, but there are some things even I
wouldn't do. And you've done them all. Tell your
people to stay the fuck away from me."

"You will need our help," Grace said. "Lia hasn't
been wrong yet."

"Listen to me, you dumb fuck!" I yelled. "I will not
turn! Not today, tomorrow, or fucking ever! Know
why? 'Cause I'll end myself before I ever cross that
line."

The psi-hacker looked away for a half-moment.

I knew that look. It was the one she got when
receiving an encrypted call. Wherever we were, I'm
sure bunches of ArgoKnights were on the other side of
the door. Part of me wanted them to breach. After all,
they took my kid from me. Left me alone in this world.

I hoped to God they breached.

"We're done then?" Grace asked. "No more
helping each other out?"

I met her gaze for a moment.

"Malcolm's still a hot target," I replied. "Without
his dad and the psi-link they shared, he'll die. Expect
his vitals to go to shit within a few hours."

"You killed his father?!" Grace gasped.

Rather than lie, I kept talking.

"I've seen this before," I gruffly assured them. "All
you have to do is bring in the right healers and a good
telepath to stabilize his mind. Keep the kid moving and
he might not fall into the wrong hands. And for fuck's
sakes, don't recruit him!"

"Why not?" Grace asked, giving away the fact that
the idea's been discussed.

I rolled my eyes.

"Let's say I'm a high-end crime boss who knows his potential. When 'Super Malcolm' pops up in an ArgoKnight uniform, I'd snatch and sell his genetic material to the highest bidder."

Forecast and Grace shared worried glances. I shrugged and paced toward my former daughter.

"That's just one scenario," I continued. "Hell! Give Teke a month. The old man could take over the kid's psi-link and turn Malcolm into a living amplifier."

I cracked my back, relieved to be 100% again. I ran my tongue over the new teeth, which had all grown in.

"If he was so inclined," I continued, "Teke could simply kill everyone and keep the planet to himself. Or, he could just kill everyone named Bob."

I paused, hoping that any of this had sunk in.

"Have I made my point?"

"Yes," Grace quietly replied.

"Good. Now, for the good of humanity, I'd suggest that you put a bullet in that kid's head and incinerate the body. Since you won't, guard him with your worthless lives and expect him to be taken anyway."

We stood in silence for several moments as the invisible ties between us withered and died.

"To answer your question, Grace," I said. "Yeah. We're done."

Grace gave me a sad smile as she held out her hand. "It was fun while it lasted."

Instead of shaking the psi-hacker's hand (or slicing it off), I looked over at my former child.

"Speak for yourself," I replied, right before the lights went out.

CHAPTER THIRTEEN

Along with the abrupt darkness, a sudden nausea rolled through my insides. It felt like standing in front of a giant speaker—while being tased. The god-awful sensation lasted a few seconds, and then went away.

My first thought was that the ArgoKnights set off some kind of trap. Gritting my teeth, I reached for my blade, ready to throw down . . . until I heard shouts of pain from the other side of the door. Guess that was Grace's backup team.

Forecast and Grace didn't look so good, either. Whatever hit me hit them too—only worse. Grace stumbled back against the wall, her hands to her temples. Forecast was on her knees and vomiting on the carpet.

"What was that?!" Forecast coughed.

"Some precog you are," I groaned.

Grace closed her eyes and tapped her ability.

"Power's out all over the complex," she reported. "I've got nothing."

Unbothered by the utter blackness, I watched the growing fear on their faces. Clearly, they weren't behind this. So who was? I slid the wakizashi back into its scabbard—for now. Grace's eyes suddenly widened with realization and fear.

"Oh God!" Grace gasped. "Cly! Get her out of–"

The psi-hacker suddenly fell to the floor, flopping around like a trout out of water. Her eyes widened from intense pain as they senselessly looked up through the darkness.

"Grace? Grace?!" Forecast panicked, unable to see shit.

I knelt over the psi-hacker and held her down, half-hoping that the bitch was merely a tongue-swallowing epileptic.

"What's wrong with her?" Forecast asked from behind me.

"No idea," I replied.

The door was kicked inward. I spun toward it, ready to kick the shit out of . . . Glue?! The super now wore an ArgoKnight uniform, complete with utility sash and a pair of sensor goggles over his eyes. While he was armed with a kinetic blaster, he had it lowered. Behind him, five uniformed ArgoKnights (the rest of his team) rushed off into the darkness. They were in their twenties and trying to hide their fear with bravado.

Judging from the ArgoKnight team badge, Glue had worked his way out of Support Staff as well. Snatching Malcolm wasn't an O'Flernan matter. It must've been an ArgoKnight op; some kind of risky, high-priority mission that (in my opinion) could've been handled better. When this was over, I'd have to find out what the stakes were.

"Grace! Forecast!" Glue hissed as he quickly moved in. "Sound off!"

Clearly unable to see, Glue's sensor goggles must've been on the fritz. That's scary. The goggles were specifically hardened against negation pulses. I stood up as Glue bumped into me. His knee-jerk reaction was to rifle butt me across the jaw. Without my mask on, the blow stung for a few seconds . . . and then I was healed up again.

"Ow," I muttered with a low voice.

"Who's there?!" Glue shouted as he slipped into a fighting stance.

By now, the ArgoKnight should've used his power on me (I would've). An adhesion field would've pinned my feet to the carpet and given him slightly better odds in a fight.

"It's Cly, dipshit," I muttered. "Touch me again and I'll sell your body to science."

"Where's Grace?" Glue asked, still on his guard.

"Having some kind of seizure," I replied. "Fuck if I know why."

I winced as Forecast popped a fiercely bright mini-flare. Under the orange light, Glue stepped back, able to see everyone clearly now.

"I haven't had any visions," Forecast confessed. "What about your power?"

"No dice," Glue frowned.

"We got hit with some kind of broad-spectrum inhibitor pulse," I theorized, relieved that my mutation had given me a resistance to such attacks.

"We need to evac," Glue told Forecast as he pulled off the sensor goggles and tossed them aside. "An assault team's gonna hit this place any second!"

"Dumb idea," I replied.

"Shut up, Cly!" Glue snapped. "We have protocols for this kind of intrusion."

"You mean the Escape Protocols in Chapter Nineteen of your fucking manual?" I scoffed. "The one about escape tunnels?"

Glue looked over at me with surprise.

"There are tons of black market copies," Forecast shrugged as she nervously glanced at the darkened doorway. "Shouldn't we be getting attacked right now?"

"No," I sighed. "They're waiting."

"For what?" Forecast asked.

"Three possibilities," I shrugged. "The shooters could be waiting for everyone to scurry into the escape tunnels. They make such perfect bottlenecks—"

A half-second later, the shooting started. Automatic weapons—lots of them—roared in the background. Grace's convulsions suddenly stopped. Forecast gently touched her neck.

"She's still got a pulse," Forecast yelled over the gunfire and sporadic explosions.

"What's the second reason?" Glue asked.

"The inhibitor pulse is so powerful that it might take a few minutes to dissipate," I reasoned. "Once it does, they'll hit us with supers."

I nodded toward the gunplay.

"The third reason's that they want to isolate their high-value targets before they kill everyone else."

"Like Malcolm?" Glue asked.

"Only if you were stupid enough to bring him here," I accusingly replied with a glance at Forecast. She confirmed my suspicion with a nod.

"Guess you were planning to recruit him after all, eh?"

The two ArgoKnights' faces fell.

"Well, it looks like Malcolm's gonna become a first-rate super villain someday," I assessed.

"They don't have him yet," Forecast replied as she scooped up Grace's Uzi.

Ah, the spunk on that kid.

"What is this place, anyway?" I asked.

"An abandoned mall in New Jersey," Glue replied after a moment's hesitation. "Gratte turned it into our main training academy."

The shooting somewhat diminished. Had I been running this op, everyone would've been using silencers. Of course, maybe these assholes wanted to add to the confusion.

"How many of you were there?" I asked.

"Sixty-eight students, along with twenty-one instructors and staff," he replied.

I tried to use Anywhere's power to teleport us out. To my annoyance, nothing happened. I casually took off my right glove. While I pretended to massage my "aching" jaw, I gazed myself. The inhibitor field had stripped away all of the powers I had stolen tonight. My shadow mutation was running just fine. Thankfully, my power rip and gaze abilities were equally unfucked.

"We'll need a new evac plan," I told them. "In another minute or two, we'll be the only ones left."

All of a sudden, Grace's eyes shot open. Glowing a bright, icy blue, they turned toward us with a hungry gleam as the psi-hacker slowly rose without a hint of pain.

"Grace! You okay?" Glue asked as he started to move toward her.

I grabbed his arm and shoved him back.

"What?!" he asked.

"Stay behind me," I said as Grace stood up and stalked toward us like a hungry carnivore.

I gazed Grace Lexia and realized that her instability was off its chain. Back in the day, it was barely visible. Whenever I gazed Grace, I saw her psi-hacking ability and "something else" lurking in the background. Now, it was plain as day and oh-so-scary.

The instability was sentient and had taken over Grace's body. In terms of psychic monstrosities, the instability and I were distant cousins. My mutation was a mix of shadow powers and predatory psychic abilities. Hers was predatory as well, with some psi-hacking thrown in. Physically, she had every edge I did— perhaps more.

All these years, Grace had somehow managed to keep the predatory side at bay. Unable to rid herself of it, she locked the thing within her mind and used it to boost her psi-hacking. That was the worst part, because the monster within had a decade to watch and learn.

If we went at it, hand-to-hand, I'd lose.

"Grace?" Forecast asked as she and Glue wisely backed away.

If Grace heard the kid, she didn't care. Her eyes were locked on mine as she sniffed me from five feet away. The choice was to either rip her or try to run (which I couldn't do). Malcolm was in the building. If those two psyches collided . . .

"Fuck!" I scowled as I plowed into Grace.

Stronger or not, she was still only a buck-twenty and easy to tackle. As I slammed her into the floor, she grabbed my throat with both hands and started to rip my mind. Caught in her choking grip, I felt a hellish mix of stinging and burning agony. Like someone set me on fire while repeatedly stabbing me. As much as I wanted to pry myself loose, I couldn't fucking move. The world started to spin through blinding pain as Grace fed on my mind.

Another second and I'd be—

Suddenly (mercifully), Grace shrieked and fell backwards as she let go. Her brand-new chest wounds didn't appear to be fatal. I scrambled back as my own mutation healed me. Odds were that her wounds were closing just as quickly. Instead of attacking the shooter, she came at me again (hungry for seconds). My right kick to her gut sent Grace flying—minus her instability. Like I did with Anywhere, I managed to rip her power mid-strike.

Grace Lexia bounced off a far wall and hit the floor unconscious.

I felt the entity's raging malice flow through me. Its alien thoughts surged forward and tried to brush aside my own. My eyes glowed that same bluish light. No longer chained to her psi-hacking ability, her damned power was so intense that I could barely turn it off. Even as I did, I sadly realized that it wouldn't stay off. The glow instantly extinguished as Forecast lowered the Uzi.

"What the fuck was that?!" she asked, justifiably freaked out.

"Your vision coming true," Glue replied with a worried glance my way. "The inhibitor pulse shut off Grace's implants. They were the only things keeping her instability at bay."

"Implants? Instabilities? What are you talking about?" Forecast asked.

I guess Grace hadn't told her about the dark side of her psi-hacking ability. Forecast regarded me with confusion.

"Grace was a latent psi-hacker," I swiftly explained. "She got caught in a bombing ten years ago. The trauma brought out her psi-hacking . . . along with a psychic instability. She's repressed it via Outfitter-made implants; which just got fried by the inhibitor pulse."

"Any other way to keep it in check?" she asked. "Paucium injections? An inhibitor collar?"

"Nothing worked," Glue replied as he slowly shook his head. "She's even tried nanite therapy, Cly. That thing's gonna bust out and take you over."

If that happened, Grace's little monster would take my body out for a campaign of wanton slaughter. Most instabilities were merely destructive. They took over their hosts and raised hell until they were put down. A rare few—like Grace's—were destructive *and* hungry. In such instances, the instabilities took over their hosts and then drank the minds of everyone they killed. Each kill had to be close (within a few yards) to work.

"How long can you hold it down?" Glue asked.

"Minutes, at best," I replied with a slight shudder in my voice. "When I lose it, I'll kill and feed on everyone I come across."

Boosted by the instability, I might end up an Omega-level threat. If it ripped and/or fed on Malcolm . . .

"Guess I do become a monster after all," I conceded with a glance at Grace.

Via the flare's light, I spotted a shadow in the corner of the room. Just large enough for us to crawl through, I used it to create a shadow tunnel.

"Uzi," I said with an outstretched hand.

Forecast hesitated for a few seconds before tossing it over. I caught it with my left hand and walked over to Grace.

"Here's the plan," I said as I grabbed the back of the psi-hacker's belt and dragged her toward the shadow tunnel. "Gunrack's gotta get those implants back online. Grace still has her psi-hacking for whatever it's worth."

"How can you be sure?" Glue asked.

"I just am," I replied with a glance at Forecast, pleased and surprised that she kept my gaze a secret. "Then, as much as I hate to admit it, you've gotta clamp a Mark-10 inhibitor collar around my neck."

Her eyes widened with hope. "Please tell me you brought it."

I dropped Grace at the edge of the shadow tunnel. Then I pulled out the mostly-reassembled Mark-10 collar from my coat pocket.

"It doesn't work," Glue reminded us as I tossed it to Forecast.

"Find Diglet, Speck, or Gunrack," I told them. "They'll know what to do."

"Go with her, Forecast," Glue ordered. "Assemble a response team and hit this site hard."

"What about you?" Forecast asked.

"I'll back up Cly," Glue said.

Glue had a pair after all. I gently kicked Grace through the tunnel. The destination was Gunrack's lab. I heard a thud as Grace fell out of the tunnel and hit the floor. Alarms began to sound off (part of Gunrack's defensive system). Since Grace was a "friendly," the security grid wouldn't kill her outright.

I doubt I'd be so lucky.

"Where's it lead?" Forecast asked.

"Gunrack's," I replied. "Keep in mind that if you cut my powers off—or kill me—the instability should instantly return to her skull. Glue, go with her."

He shook his head.

"Aside from the fact I don't trust you, Cly, this ain't a one-man op. You can be the distraction while I find Malcolm and get him out of here."

He had a point.

"I'd be tempted to let you tag along," I grudgingly admitted. "Too bad you're helpless."

To make my point, I easily snatched Glue by his utility sash and lifted him off his feet. He dropped the useless energy weapon and (laughingly) tried to pry free of my grip.

"What the hell are you doing?!" Glue grunted.

"Ending this discussion," I replied before throwing him into the shadow tunnel like he was an oversized teddy bear.

I turned toward Forecast.

"What about the other trainees?" she asked. "I could help."

Amidst the sounds of death and mayhem outside, the answer was obvious.

"They're extinct," I muttered.

The shooting slowed down. A girl's scream was cut short by something or someone.

"Besides, this changes nothing between us," I scowled. "Nothing."

Forecast started to leave. Then she stopped and turned.

"I did what I thought was right," she stubbornly replied. "Can't you see that?!"

"I know," I replied with a quiet, spiteful grin. "Just remember something: this is your fault. Had you trusted me, we might've prevented this. Instead, a whole generation of heroes are dead—heroes you could've saved."

Forecast blinked through my harsh logic. She started to say something else when I stumbled back a step.

"Dad?" she rushed over and knelt beside me.

I dropped to a knee as my insides began to churn. A sudden wave of unrelenting hunger hit me. It wanted me to turn the power back on. To let it loose. Back when I was ripping minds, the urge to feed was always difficult to deny. But this . . . this was insane. Sweat began to form on me as I turned to Forecast. The kid's mind smelled terrified and fresh.

"Get ghost!" I trembled.

Forecast hesitantly nodded.

Then she ran toward the tunnel, did a baseball slide, and disappeared from view. I closed it and set the Uzi down. With trembling hands, I put my mask back on. My right hand picked up the Uzi. The left drew the wakizashi as I stood up and forced a deep breath through my lungs.

A plan came to mind—a bad one.

I ran down the narrow service corridor, toward the main area of the mall. Ahead of me was a pair of metal doors. On the other side, my sensitive ears heard a woman whispering into a radio. I reversed my grip on the wakizashi and stabbed through the right door in a downward angle. Killed in mid-sentence, I guess I had thrown away the element of surprise and a free psychic lunch.

Fair enough.

Right now, my simple objective was to grab Malcolm and throw him into a shadow tunnel before these fuckers took me down. Anyone here to wipe out a bunch of fledgling ArgoKnights should (hopefully) have more than enough muscle to stop me. That meant surrendering to the first bunch of shooters I found.

The idea offended the pro in me. It was a reckless, stupid plan. There wasn't an exit strategy or hope of rescue. Still, it beat the alternative where I'd become a monster and go on a psychic rampage through Jersey. The only thing I knew for certain was that they weren't here for Malcolm.

A raid this major had to have been planned well in advance. They might've been here to snuff the site or grab Grace, who had priceless intel in her head. Whatever their objective, Malcolm was simply a bonus—assuming they wanted him alive.

I was even more of a catch. My DNA was worth a ton of cash in the right circles (especially if they took me alive). As a former fixer, my secrets were valuable and worth carving out of me. Hell, with a bit of brainwashing, they might even flip me into quite the loyal minion—

Then I felt the instability surge again and knew that I was low on time. I pulled my blade free, opened the doors, and eyed my latest kill.

CHAPTER FOURTEEN

The dead merc was facedown and bleeding from a hole through her neck. Seeing as mercs tended to run in packs, I was surprised to find her alone. Maybe she got cut off from her unit. Or perhaps, with a complex this large, they spread their forces a bit too thin.

After sheathing the wakizashi, I flipped her over with my left boot. Almost attractive, her lifeless eyes stared up at me through black camo paint. Her blondish hair was tied up in a bun underneath a black beret. Maybe in her late thirties, she looked like a standard gun-for-hire. Only, her gear was too high-end.

I sized up her unmarked black fatigues and assorted op tech. Armed with a fancy assault rifle, she looked to be part of a serious corporate firm. There were plenty of these outfits around. While not as good as my firm once was, they tended to make up for a lack of quality with an abundance of trained cannon fodder.

My power gaze pegged her as human. Across her flat bosom was a half-empty combat harness. I plucked a tube flare, popped it, and then rolled it into a darkened corner of the doorway. Beyond the doors was what appeared to be a set of bathrooms and then the food court.

"Bravo Six?!" A worried male voice replied from her earpiece. "Bravo Six, respond!"

Guess he heard her die. I set the Uzi down. With a grin, I picked up the tiny plastic device and one of her frag grenades.

"Sorry, Shithead One," I mocked. "Bravo Six is bleeding all over my boots. Maybe you should get out while you still can."

"Who is this?!" Shithead One barked as I opened a shadow tunnel along the floor near me.

Most people assumed that I had to know someone's face in order to shadowport to them. Actually, a voice worked just fine. Scents were much harder.

"Don't worry about me, motherfucker," I replied as I pulled the pin. "Worry about yourself."

With a Grinch-like smile, I dropped the grenade through the tunnel and stepped back. The explosive clattered out of the other end. I left it open and savored the screams of panic. I could hear rotors in the background—larger than that fucking news chopper's. Then the grenade went off.

A bit of the fiery blast erupted through the shadow tunnel. Warning sirens blared, which suggested a pending crash. More screams. I smiled in anticipation. Then a distant, powerful explosion raged above the complex. A few seconds later, something crashed on the other side of the ex-mall. It was enough to make the whole place shake.

Deprived of its source shadow, the other end of my portal closed on its own. I tossed the earpiece, fairly certain that I had fucked up again. Should've just surrendered. Instead, I pretty much made sure that they'd kill me. Well . . . fuck 'em. Any outfit this lame didn't deserve to catch the likes of me.

Via the flare's steady light, I opened a new shadow portal and angled it toward Malcolm, quietly hoping that the kid was dead by now. Instead, I heard sobbing and rolled my tired eyes. This kid had more lives than Christ!

Instead of rushing in, I picked up Grace's Uzi and cautiously peeked through the portal. He was hiding in an oversized swimming area. Five bodies—all boys—were floating in it. Shot to shit, their blood had covered a sizeable portion of the surface water. Whoever butchered these trainees had set an ArgoKnight flag on fire. That act of spite provided me with the shadow I needed to enter the otherwise-darkened room.

I looked around for the source of the sobbing.

On the far-left side was a set of bleachers. Malcolm's pitiful sobs echoed from behind it. I had to remind myself that this was a civilian—a kid without a lick of training. Odds were that he couldn't kill anything bigger than a bug. When I was his age, I already had a few dozen kills under my belt.

Didn't even have my augments yet.

I slowly crawled out of the burning flag's shadow and crept around the bleachers. Drenched in water, Malcolm sat in a pair of gray trunks. Staring at his dead pool buddies, he didn't hear me coming. By the time he sensed my approach, I clamped my free hand over his mouth and stifled his terrified screams.

"Quiet!" I hissed. "I'm getting you out of here. Understand?"

The kid nodded. I removed my hand. Breathing hard, it took Malcolm a moment to recognize me from Meadows Park. Guess I had grimed up since we last saw each other.

"Are you okay?" he asked.

"I'm fine," I frowned, bothered by his sincere concern. "You?"

Malcolm shook his head—

A cold surge of hunger rushed through me. Malcolm's mind . . . it was like sitting in front of a perfect meal after days without food. Even better was the fact that I hated this fucking kid. Like the rest of his damned family, this little Irish shithead had cost me everything.

Had Glue not driven this boy into my city, I wouldn't have known about Lia's betrayal. She'd still be my daughter and Gunrack would still be my woman. Because of this bastard son, I was all alone. Maybe . . .

maybe it was better that way. I could be a lone hunter without obligations, lost causes, and betrayals to concern me.

The realization was utterly tempting.

I *was* better off alone. After these past few months, the need for human contact had made me weak. It was best dealt with by feeding. Each mind I ate could quench that need for contact because I'd know that person. Why make friends when I could simply eat their minds?

The logic didn't seem so odd right now.

Fuck being a hero, boyfriend, or even a father. I was a killer. Ending this kid (and the threat he posed) would make the food chain a safer place. Then I'd feed on the ArgoKnights, Harlot, and anyone else who threatened me. I'd make the world fear me. No one would ever fuck with me again—

"How do we get out of here?" Malcolm nervously asked, bothered by the way I was staring at him.

I so wanted to flip on the instability and drink this kid's mind. The kid had so much untapped psychic energy that I might never need to feed again. Yeah, that made sense. I could kill two birds with one Malcolm.

"Mister?" Malcolm asked. "You sure you're okay?"

It could be that simple. So simple. I just had to turn the power back on and let it out.

Let it out . . .

I looked into Malcolm's innocent eyes and—

"I'm fine," I lied. "We have to move. Now."

I wasn't gonna break one of my oldest rules; not even for a bastard son with rotten luck. The instability howled from deep inside of my mind (in Grace's voice). *LET. ME. OUT!* The voice echoed so loudly in my skull that it staggered me for a moment.

"This way," I told Malcolm as I headed for the flag.

The kid wiped away his tears and followed me.

Give him to me and you'll never be weak again, it seductively offered. *We'll crush your enemies and make them beg for death. Start with the child! You'd be unstoppable!*

I didn't bother to reply. Talking to a dead mobster was weird enough. Chatting with someone else's psychic trauma was a bit much. *No children, no feds.* One of the core principles of my time as a fixer. Ignore your principles and you were nothing. Besides, if I cut on the instability, it might eat my mind first and then make Malcolm into the main course.

What to do? What to do?

"Where are we going?" Malcolm asked, probably wondering why we were heading toward a burning flag.

"Escape route," I replied. "Come on."

As the kid came within arm's reach I had a new idea. I gently grabbed Malcolm's arm and ripped his psi-link. The little fucker would be less dangerous with it. It might also give me a Plan B.

Release me!

"Ever been to Miami?" I asked.

Malcolm shook his head as I let him go.

"It's like Malibu," I shrugged as I took off my mask. "Just more humid."

I opened up a new shadow portal. Teke was on the other end.

Another lifetime ago, my former mentor was an Army colonel. Even though he had just turned sixty-two, Teke still had the body of a ten-year-old. A bizarre genetic disorder kept him looking like a child for the last fifty-two years. Said disorder also amplified his psychic powers, making him one of the most powerful telepaths in the world.

Teke recruited, trained, and commanded me during our black ops days. He had seen more covert actions, wars, and mayhem than I ever would. Had he killed me in '99, like he had been ordered to, Teke would've been able to retire in style. Instead, he had to go into hiding.

Framed for treason, Teke had gotten his face and skin color altered. The result was that he now looked like an adorable little black kid with nappy hair. Once I made it in the fixer game, I hired Teke for the sole purpose of protecting him. He did lightweight work for me and got paid (too much) for his efforts. The biggest regret about losing my firm was that I couldn't protect him anymore.

After that HydroNemesis thing, Teke opted to leave Pillar City and relocate to a suburban Miami condo. His stated goal was to actually retire. Granted, if certain parties knew he was alive, Teke would've ended up assassinated—or worse. Anyone with as many enemies as he did should've been worried. Then again, the old man was too cool to give a fuck.

Dressed in a red pair of silk pajamas, Teke reclined on a brown leather couch. A small bottle of German microbrew rested on a nearby coffee table. Enjoying a soccer game on a large plasma TV, he abruptly sensed our minds and looked up. Rather than ask me what the fuck was going on, he narrowed his eyes and gave my mind a casual once-over. Normally, I'd let Teke in (out of trust). Now, I had to keep my mind locked down or Grace's instability would kill us all.

Teke took the hint and kept things verbal.

"Hey, old man," I said, with a forced smile.

Free me!

Teke looked Malcolm over. His jaw then dropped.

"What shit are you leaving on my doorstep?!" Teke asked, his voice still like a boy's.

"A patch job," I replied as Malcolm nervously looked up at me. "Malcolm, Teke. Teke, Malcolm. He'll keep an eye on you while I clean up this mess."

The O'Flernan yelped as I shoved him through the portal. Without even a twitch, Teke caught Malcolm with his telekinesis and gently lowered him to the carpeted floor. The old man gave his guest a curt nod and then looked back at me.

"He's just exited a long-term psychic symbiosis," I warned Teke, "Rehab his mind, find him a good healer, and give him a combat package."

"Why bother?" Teke frowned. "He's an Omega. Wouldn't a bullet to the head make more sense?"

Malcolm gawked up at me, clearly having doubts about his new babysitter.

"That's what you get for giving me a killer's ethics," I replied with a wry grin. "Send me a bill."

"It'll be huge," Teke promised with a surly yawn. "I'll call Anywhere and have him send someone."

"No you won't," I told him. "Leave the ArgoKnights, Grace, and Forecast out of this."

Teke's left eyebrow arched at the mention of Lia's old call sign. "You have a falling out?"

"And then some," I replied. "Do not trust them."

The old telepath thoughtfully nodded.

"Mind if I call in a certain redneck?"

Teke was referring to Dirtnap, another one of my former employees. Georgia-born and fast with a gun, he was almost as good a shot as Pinpoint. Stuck with the mixed blessings of a large family, he was chasing freelance bounties to pay the bills. One of Dirtnap's gigs must've brought him to the Miami area.

"Sure" I replied. "Offer him way too much."

"I will," Teke replied as he got up. "Have a seat, kid. I'll try to find something that'll fit you."

Seeing as Malcolm was a head taller than Teke, I doubted that was gonna happen. Malcolm reluctantly sat on the couch.

Let me out!

"You gonna be okay?" Teke asked with genuine concern.

"This is worse than last October," I earnestly replied.

"That was nothing!" Teke scoffed. "Remember that infestation we stopped in Panama? Now *that* was real danger."

Teke had a point.

"Remember Grace's little problem?" I asked as I tapped my skull. "It's mine now."

"Oh," he muttered with restrained dread.

If Teke was white he'd have turned pale. Normally, he'd have my back. This was different. To a telepath, fighting a hungry instability was like fighting a fire while drenched in gasoline.

"If I survive, I'll swing by and tell you all about it."

My mentor swallowed hard. "Just be yourself, Cly. The rest'll work itself out."

In spite of everything, I grinned. It was good to have someone (anyone) believe in me right now. I nodded, hoping that our next reunion wouldn't be in a funeral home.

"Well," Teke shrugged. "I'll throw some beers in the fridge. Pick him up by noon, eh? I've got a lunch date tomorrow."

"How old is she?" I asked, sweating from the strain.

"A gentleman never tells," Teke replied as the beer floated into his hand.

The old telepath took a swig of his brew and then toasted me farewell as I closed the portal. I wanted to believe that Malcolm would be safe on the other side. Of course, I knew otherwise—

Let me out!

This damned thing was getting on my fucking nerves. Without her implants, Grace would've given in to this thing years ago. Another minute and I might break too. It was like having a full bladder (but in my psyche). This thing was gonna bust out, whether I wanted it to or not. So, I decided to do this on my terms . . .

I put the Uzi to my head.

"Stop fighting me—right now—or I pull the trigger."

I heard it laugh inside my mind as it continued to vie for dominance.

Kill yourself. Then I'll return to Grace and have full control.

I scornfully laughed. "A million bucks says that Grace Lexia is locked in a stasis bed by now. Probably the same one they had set aside for me. I'd also wager that they've slipped her a mind pill and a whole lot of Paucium. Hell, Gunrack might've even strapped a bomb to her head—just in case."

You fucker, it hissed.

Glue wasn't stupid. Neither was my kid. Whatever containment protocols they had set up for me were already in place. They could be quickly modified to contain Grace. I'm sure I've bought them more than enough time to lock her away. The instability's push to take over subsided . . . for now.

"Much better," I sighed as I lowered the Uzi. "Now, let's come up with a more suitable arrangement."

I'm hungry, it impatiently reminded me. *You remember what that's like.*

"I do. I really do," I replied. "Here's the deal. We link up."

Like Connor O'Flernan and his scared little child?

Judging from its tone, the instability didn't want to be a second-class citizen in my head. Neither did I.

"More like I let you roam free."

My head was silent for several moments.

I'm listening.

CHAPTER FIFTEEN

"First thing's first," I said as I sat down on the bullet-riddled bleachers.

What's that?

"You need a name," I muttered as I looked over at the floating bodies in the pool. "Unless you want to be called 'Grace's Hungry Instability.'"

You have a point, it replied. *Call me . . . Reckoner.*

"I like it. Okay, Reckoner, what do you want?"

To feed.

"And then what?" I asked. "Kill too many victims at once, folks are gonna notice. The only way they won't care is if you kill *right kind of victim*—fuckers no one'll miss."

The notion made it chuckle.

You suggest becoming a vigilante?

"Something like that," I replied, wishing I had my smokes. "If you kill the worst of the worst, people might even pay you."

The instability went silent for several moments.

Why should I serve you?

"You wouldn't," I replied. "You're the psychic dark side of a decorated ex-cop. Don't tell me the idea of putting down killers and rapists doesn't appeal."

Who would I target?

"You tell me," I shrugged. "How much of Grace's memories do you have?"

All of them. And a few of my own.

"How many of them could use some vigilante justice, right now?"

How can you trust me? Especially after tonight?

"Doesn't matter," came my candid reply. "You'll do this because there's no other choice. You're old enough—and smart enough—to see the angles. The world's low on crime fighters. If you kill enough bad guys, the ArgoKnights just might leave you alone. Fuck! They might even offer you a job."

You don't seriously believe that, it hissed.

"They tried to recruit me, remember?" I smiled as I leaned forward and tapped my chest. "Things are so fucking bad that I'm fighting crime. *Me!*"

I could feel the instability considering it.

"You might wanna save the world a few times, while you're at it," I continued.

The instability was silent for several seconds.

Even if I took your offer seriously, why should I risk my freedom—or my life?

"If everyone dies," I patiently explained, "there goes your food supply. You have to protect us. Having sat in Grace's head, you've seen the same threats. Someone like you could make a difference."

I'll never be an ArgoKnight, it bitterly vowed. *Never!*

"Then just be the Reckoner," I shrugged. "Do it right and you might kick more ass than they ever could. Think it over."

I carefully set the Uzi on my lap and stared off into the darkened murder scene. I could do the right thing and kill this thing. Lives would be saved, blah-blah-blah. Of course, it was the ultimate archive; with more vital intel in its head than (arguably) any computer network in the world. Reckoner intimately knew every threat to mankind that Grace had discovered in the last decade.

Killing it might kill us all.

Cross me and you're dead, it finally said.

"Likewise," I replied.

Now, how are you going to let me out?

"By giving you a body of your own."

155 · Murder Sauce

With that, I allowed Grace's instability to leave my skull. Fueled by Malcolm's psi-link, it was able to manifest. While not as powerful as Connor was, the instability popped into existence. It looked just like Grace Lexia; down to the clothes she was wearing at the time.

Reckoner had no scent and didn't breathe. When it moved, it barely made a sound. I tossed it the Uzi. The instability caught the weapon and then eyed me, weighing odds as only a proper villain would.

"Perfection," I softly applauded.

Even with the hunger on its face, Reckoner managed a polite nod.

"Thank you," it smiled, pleased with the sound of its (Grace's) voice.

Then it whipped its head toward the doorway with a dangerous smile.

"Food!" it hissed, sensing living minds.

I could hear the stealthy approach of three—no, four—hostiles. Coming on my right, they were on the other side of the large room.

"Now go make a name for yourself," I urged. "You should probably spare any innocent types you come across. Just a thought."

"Fine!" Reckoner impatiently glanced at me. "Can I kill them now?!"

"Oh, sorry. Go right ahead."

The mercs burst through the door right as Reckoner opened fire. The Uzi's barrel flashed at full-auto. The mercs barely got a shot off before they died. A few bullets harmlessly ricocheted off her energy form. Through our psi-link, I could feel four screaming minds devoured by Reckoner.

An almost-forgotten part of me craved the "taste" of the ripped minds. Fortunately, Reckoner consumed every scrap of their psychic energy. Could I have fed on them? As tempting as it was to try, I didn't dare. Not only would I fall off the wagon, Reckoner might turn on me. I severed the link, rather than give in to the temptation.

Reckoner turned toward me with a suspicious glance.

"You severed the link."

"You've had enough of my psyche for one day," I muttered, tired from the psychic strain of the last few minutes.

Reckoner gave me a grateful nod. A bit surprised by the monster's gratitude, I returned the gesture. I so wanted to gaze its power(s) but I didn't dare. My power gaze was (after all) psychic in nature. Using it on Reckoner would be like pouring blood into a shark tank. It could sense my gaze, think I had reneged on our deal, and then kill me.

I would.

"You full?" I asked, knowing that it wasn't.

"For now," Reckoner lied with a smile.

Instabilities were never sated. Aside from overwhelming psychic damage, the only way to kill Reckoner would be to starve it of psychic energy. In its shoes, I'd kill every motherfucker in here.

After Reckoner's brief burst of gunplay, we both knew that more mercs would show up. With that thing out of my head, I didn't have to do anything noble. In fact, I kinda wanted to take a nap right now.

"Well, this has been fun," I said as I stood up and turned away from Reckoner. "Drop me a call if you need anything."

The burning flag was beginning to dim. I headed toward it and opened a shadow portal back to the loft. I felt its disbelieving eyes on me as I walked into the shadow.

"Wait," Reckoner frowned.

Halfway into my loft, I stopped and turned.

"You're not going to find out who sent these scumbags or why?!"

I stopped and pretended to think about it.

"Nope," I replied with a fake sigh of regret. "Too bad there's not a skilled investigator out there; someone with the brains, balls, and the power to stop their nefarious scheme. Oh, woe is us—"

"I get it! I get it!" Reckoner groaned. "Fine. I'll look into this mess for you."

"Thanks," I replied. "Shoot me an e-mail, huh?"

Reckoner nodded as it dropped the empty SMG and headed for the mercs. Clearly, it planned to *Rambo* up a bit before more mercs/victims/food arrived.

"And Reckoner?" I paused, a dead-serious look on my face.

"Yeah?"

"If you end up with a book deal, a reality show, or even your own coffee mug . . . I want a percentage."

The instability gave me a smile (and the finger) as I left the room.

I stepped out of the moonlit shadows of my loft's bedroom and immediately headed for the closet. It was large enough to hold the spare tools of my trade. First, I emptied my pockets. Everything was smashed—except for the diamonds, spare cash, and my lucky condom, all of which I kept. I pitched my utility harness and grabbed my pre-loaded spare. Then I went for a fresh pack of Marlboros, a new lighter, two new burner phones, and a pair of Glock .45's. I also replaced my ruined watch.

Once I geared up, I headed for the bathroom and commenced to brushing the coppery taste of blood from my mouth. My mirror had been shattered by the screecher grenade. Probably for the best. I'm sure that the sight of my reflection would've made me cringe. Instead of a much-needed shower, I had to head right back out. There was just too much shit to get done. I poured myself some Listerine—

—and that's when Connor (the idiot) tried to take over my mind. I was stone-tired and mentally taxed. After the inhibitor pulse, I no longer had the SWAP cop's stolen mind powers. Had he waited until I went to sleep, Connor might've gotten me. Instead, he "jumped" me whilst I was gargling. The entity laughed at the idea of beating me . . . until I held him back.

I'm starting to hate you less and less, Cly.

I spat out the mouthwash and set my cup down.

"Stop trying to take over," I muttered, as the entity tried to wrestle my angry mind into submission.

Or you'll do wha-AAARRRRGGGHHHHH!

I fed him a brief sample platter of the most agonizing moments in my life. Having been psi-trained by the best, I knew how to play with unwanted guests in my head. It was a basic prerequisite for superhuman black ops. Weakened from tonight's violence, Connor instantly backed off.

AlrightAlright!

I stopped the onslaught. My "guest" needed a few seconds to compose his thoughts.

So what now?

"I'm gonna explain a few things to you," I said as I headed through the living room and toward my broken window.

"First off, you're a very temporary guest," I muttered as my boots crunched over broken glass.

Then I hopped out of the window and dropped seven stories with Connor screaming in my mind. Guess he figured that we were about to die. With my physique, the impact with the ground barely annoyed me.

"Second, I'm gonna keep you out of your kid's head."

Standing in the rear lot of my building, I eyed Harlot's unconscious shooters. My security team had left them here (bound, of course) with their op tech piled nearby. There were enough security cameras for Lou's team to easily keep an eye on these morons.

I'm his father! Connor protested. *You have no right to keep me from him.*

"You do realize that your kid's an Omega-level psychic, right?"

There was a moment of silence.

What's that?

I sighed and face-palmed myself as Lou rushed out the back door. Five seconds, give-or-take. Not a bad response time.

"Is everything all right, Mr. Cly?" he anxiously asked, looking around.

"Not by a damned sight, Lou," I sadly grinned, thinking of Forecast. "Is Gunrack still here?"

"She left in a hurry, just now," Lou replied.

Of course she did.

Glue must've called her with the bad news. Gratte would send a bunch of ArgoKnights to the Jersey site. Hopefully, Reckoner would be gone from the mall before those reinforcements arrived.

I turned toward Lou.

"Tell me about the bug sweep. You find anything?"

Lou sighed his frustration.

"No, Mr. Cly. Shall I initiate another one?"

My eyes narrowed. Harlot had acquired intimate knowledge of my security arrangements without electronic surveillance. That meant someone had sold me out—but whom?

"Don't bother," I replied. "Tell the guys to drop to a normal threat level."

Lou nodded.

"Anything else, Mr. Cly?"

"Tell Gratte that I'm fine and to warn the rescue team to stay out of the 'mall' for an hour or so. He'll understand what I mean."

Lou pulled out a cell phone.

"And, uh, pack Lia's things and send them to the *Lairs 'R Us* offices in Downtown. She no longer resides here."

Lou paused and his eyes narrowed for a moment. Then he nodded with a saddened understanding. After all, the Sicilian was from a big family. In his fifties, I'm sure one of Lou's relatives left the nest under less-than-ideal conditions.

"Should I revoke her access?"

"All levels," I replied. "Same for Gunrack and Grace. That's all."

Sensing my tired, grumpy mood, Lou reigned in his curiosity. He simply dialed Gratte and walked off.

That was harsh, Connor uncaringly remarked. *Now, what's this 'Omega-level' crap about? You're talkin' about my son like he's one of the Four Horsemen!*

I sighed my impatience.

"An Omega-level psychic is insanely powerful. In the wrong hands, your son could blow up the planet or help someone else take it over. His powers weren't actively dangerous; until you up and manifested. Doing that turned your boy into a doomsday weapon with zits."

Dead silence.

"Now," I continued, "the bad guys are gonna come after you and eventually your son. You're the ignition key for his powers. When they capture you, they can weaponize Malcolm."

So that's your plan? You want his powers?!
Connor asked with certainty in his tone.

"God, you're dumb," I sighed. "If I wanted the boy's powers, I'd just rip both of you."

Then why haven't you? Connor dubiously asked.

"Were you asleep when I said 'blow up the planet'?! I'd sooner stick a live nuke up my ass than have both of your powers at once."

There was a thoughtful pause.

So what now?

"My original plan was to let your sorry ass die," I continued. "Being in a psychic symbiosis, the kid would die with you. The world's safe. End credits."

I stalked toward Harlot's guys. Most of them were supers with interesting abilities. Judging from her choice of superhumans, Harlot wanted me alive. I wonder why? I knelt down and ripped the flight power off of a muscle-bound Wung operative. Better than a flight collar, it might be of use.

I saw what you did with that Reckoner thing, Connor said. *Can you do that for me too?*

"Glad you were paying attention," I muttered as I ripped the knowledge absorption power from a geeky little Wung. This power was a cousin of the psi-hacking ability, one where I could pull data from any inanimate object (books, computers, storage devices, etc.). Purely psychic, I had to touch the object for this ability to work. Also, I couldn't control a complex device. Still, I could grab Grace's implants and store all of that data in my brain (for the sake of posterity, of course).

C'mon, Cly! You don't want me stuck in your head forever, do ya'?

"No, I do not," came my distracted reply.

Then I grinned.

"Of course, I could just have Teke shove you out."

I'd stay out of your way, Connor begged. *And away from Malcolm too.*

Annoyed by his (lying) voice in my head, I kicked on the psi-link. Surprised, Connor tried to latch on and take over my brain again. As his energy form tumbled out of thin air, I cut the psi-link before Connor could gain any leverage. Wow! For a non-psychic, his mind was strong.

Connor looked down at his hands and realized that he was fucked. Without an energy source to sustain him, he would die. To think—he was almost unbeatable a few hours ago.

"C'mon Cly! You're supposed to be one of the good guys!" Connor pleaded.

"No I'm not," I smirked as I rose to my full height.

"We can do a deal," Connor offered. "If you leave me like this, I'm dead in a day."

"More like an hour or two," I corrected him. "My mind's not as juicy as your kid's."

Connor heard the hint of disapproval in my tone and reigned in his angry response.

"Anything you want," he offered. "Please."

I opened up my Marlboros and lit up, deep in thought. Connor waited in the background, utterly under my thumb. While I wasn't enjoying this (much), I couldn't think of any useful role for him. Still, take away his mob ties, his past attempts on my life, and the fact that he's a threat to humanity . . . and Connor O'Flernan wasn't all bad.

"Fuck it," I whispered as I dropped my cigarette butt and smushed it under my boot.

I walked over to a shadow, knelt down, and thought of the SWAP cop—the one whose nice ass I had saved. I opened a portal and found her asleep in her bed. Connor gave me a hopeful smile as I reached through. Ignoring the strain, I gently shoved my right arm out of the shadow of her hospital bed and touched her right leg. Her eyes snapped opened as I ripped her telepathy and memory powers. By the time she flipped on the lamp, I had pulled my arm out of the portal. Another second and the lamp's light would've collapsed portal and I'd be minus a limb.

"Okay, Connor, you're gonna get a psychic makeover."

"Meaning?" he frowned.

"You get to become someone else," I gestured for him to follow me toward a shadowy section of my building.

"Who?" he asked.

"Someone way the fuck cooler."

The shadow tunnel dropped us out on the convenient rooftop of an old foundry in Downtown. The sprawling site was still active, running 24/7, and nowhere near my usual haunts. While not that quiet, no one should bother us here.

"Where are we?" Connor asked.

"Shut up and lay on your back," I grumbled as I sat down. "I don't have all night."

Connor hesitated for a moment and then complied.

I let Reckoner walk away because it was too valuable to kill. Seamus' eldest son wasn't so lucky. Still, the fucker had suffered enough.

"My patience with you is just about gone," I flatly threatened. "Try any shit at all and I will kill you. Okay?"

The entity longingly looked out upon Downtown's skyline before he nodded. I tuned out the world and established the psi-link. Connor's psyche nervously waited on the other end. This time he behaved himself as I took over. First, I kicked on the telepathy and memory editing abilities. With them, I could give Connor complete amnesia or make him think he was an Elvis impersonator of Martian descent.

The plan was to rearrange his life goals. Three things had sustained him all of these years: his son's well being, dreams of revenge on Ronns, and the idea of running the O'Flernan mob. Each goal was deeply embedded into Connor's psyche.

Prying them loose took about an hour of intense psychic rearrangement.

When I was done with Connor, his desire to kill Ronns had been reduced to a general whim. Out of sight, out of mind. Still, should he ever come across Ronns again, the entity would kill him with a fair amount of glee. Also, Connor had "forgiven" me for killing Seamus; solely on the grounds that the old fucker had it coming.

Connor also trusted me to protect his fucking kid. The threat their psi-link posed couldn't be ignored, so he would never—ever—link with his kid again (no matter what). Billions of lives were more important than his paternal devotion. As for running the O'Flernan clan, Connor suddenly "realized" that it felt too much like work. That he wasn't mature enough (true) or smart enough (also true) to make it thrive. Instead, he'd just leave it alone.

I decided that Connor would want to be a freelance crook instead. The lifestyle of a charming rogue now appealed more to him than being a hot-tempered asshole. Once in a while, Connor might even be inclined to do some good in the world. Lastly, I changed his identity. From now on, he'd run under the street name of . . . "Kasper."

The funkiest thing of all? I let Connor remember that I had played with his thoughts. The fucker would simply walk away knowing that I did this for the best, which was technically true. Kasper would bounce from host-to-host, feeding (a little) on their minds as an intangible burst of psychic energy. Having fed off Malcolm since his death, the transition wasn't much of a stretch. The way he worked his son like a puppet, I figured that Kasper could even possess most non-psychics with relative ease.

"Couldn't you have picked a cooler tag?" Kasper protested aloud, still lying on his back.

All griping aside, his surface thoughts were intrigued with the new mindset and the freedom it offered. Once I released him, I knew he'd go out for a night on the town. Having gone without sex and booze for so many years, Kasper had every right to indulge.

"Casper was the 'friendly ghost,'" I explained. "You don't have to be."

"Anything else?" he chuckled.

"Good question," I muttered as I put a fresh cigarette in my mouth. "Gimme a minute."

Still seated, I lit up and reviewed my psychic handiwork. Brainwashing up a new personality was much like crafting a sword. If poorly done, my conditioning would snap under significant stress and he'd be Connor O'Flernan all over again.

Teke would've mocked some of my rougher edges. But all in all, it should hold. Another (more capable) psychic could twist up my handiwork, so I added in a general inclination to avoid them. Lastly, against my better judgment, I gave Kasper one of my permanent contact numbers (in case of emergency).

"C'mon Cly!" Kasper whined, "I need to get my freak-on!"

"All done," I replied as I stood up and walked over to the roof's edge.

Kasper hopped up and followed me. I spied a bunch of blue-collar types leaving, probably for the night.

"Pick one."

"Don't mind if I do," Kasper replied, as he went intangible and faded from my sight.

"Behave yourself," I light-heartedly warned him.

No chance of that, Cly, he whispered within my mind. *And thanks.*

I severed the psi-link.

Just like that, Connor O'Flernan was no more.

Gone from my mind, he was Kasper now. One of the departing workers paused and allowed his colleagues to walk past. He then turned and looked up at me. The mischievous grin told me that I had unleashed another rogue upon the world.

Fair enough.

CHAPTER SIXTEEN

It was 2:41 a.m. per my watch.

The stress on my brain made me want to just go back home and fucking crash. Then I thought of those dead boys in the water. Anyone who'd do that wouldn't stop until they achieved their objective(s). My guess? They were after Grace. She knew way too many secrets. Whoever had them could (without exaggeration) take over the world.

If I were their shot-caller, I wouldn't call it a night. I'd have intel on her known associates and probable safe houses. Gunrack's lab would be the first place I'd look. Even if Grace weren't there, I'd take it out of the equation anyway. Without its resources, the local ArgoKnight assets would be much easier to kill.

I should warn them. If the mercs hit the lab with another inhibitor pulse, game over. They'd have Glue, Gunrack, Forecast, and (probably) Grace. Rather than getting too involved, I could contact Anywhere and have him do a quick evac . . .

Wait a sec.

I blinked and looked at my watch again.

I left Anywhere and Pinpoint in a Downtown post office (minus the ability to teleport away). Heh! The thought made me grin. Once I teleported away with Forecast, they'd have to escape from a high-visibility crime scene (in ArgoKnight gear) with God-knew how many Pillar City cops descending on them. And there was the news chopper.

Of course, when I got nailed by the inhibitor pulse, Anywhere should've gotten his power back. Still, if he got busted, the cops would've dosed him with Paucium—or killed him outright. He and Pinpoint might need some bailing out. Normally, I'd leave the fuckers to their just desserts but Grace and her implants were too important. I'd need their help.

I glanced through the nearest shadow and looked for the backstabbing duo. My eyes narrowed at what I saw. With a scowl, I whipped out the Glocks and then dove into the expanding shadow portal. From under a corner table, I rolled along the brightly lit white linoleum of a mirrored interrogation room. I shot the nearest plain-clothes cop through the back of his skull.

Straddling Pinpoint, said cop had her pinned to the floor with his bulk. His thick fingers had been working the wrapper on a condom pack when he died. As the fucker fell off her, I sized up Pinpoint and involuntarily winced.

The ArgoKnight had been stripped down to her white bra and panties. Her face was splattered with the dead cop's blood. Her wrists were cuffed behind her. She had taken one helluva beating. Busted lip. One eye mashed shut. Her left shoulder was clearly dislocated.

Pinpoint looked up at me with utter dread, certain that I had come here to finish her off. Instead, I gunned down the two other cops in the room as they went for their guns. Before they died, the fuckers were busy beating Anywhere with old-style billy clubs. Both of the teleporter's wrists had been handcuffed to the chair. Stripped out of his uniform, they left him in a gray pair of briefs and matching socks. Knocked out-cold, blood poured out from the teleporter's mouth.

The room's one-way mirror might've had someone on the other side. Not up for taking chances, I emptied my clips through it. As the glass shattered, two more guys hit the floor (both too dead to fire their drawn handguns). Dressed in fancy suits, they didn't look like Pillar City PD. Feds, perhaps? Beyond them was a camera, which was recording the gruesome scene (God ask me why).

As I reloaded the Glocks, I wondered what they hoped to gain.

Even the feds should've known how ArgoKnight psi-screens worked. Basically unbreakable, every member was automatically psi-screened. Their version was uniquely designed so that they could be turned on/off at will. It also blocked out hostile mental intrusions, traumas, and even extreme pain.

Wait . . . maybe these assholes understood ArgoKnight psi-screens after all. The mental defense came with one major flaw. Due to the need for field flexibility, the psi-screens wouldn't prevent an ArgoKnight from *volunteering* information. My guess was that the cops were wondering who'd break first. Could Anywhere sit there and watch his friend get raped? Or would Pinpoint break first and spare the teleporter a brutal death?

After holstering my guns, I hopped into the observation room. Then I cut on the knowledge absorption power and touched the camera. My mind took in only sixteen minutes' worth of footage.

The two suits initially handled the interrogation. They identified themselves as Interpol agents, had British accents, and briefly questioned the two about their fight with me. Most of all, they wanted to know about the incident on Jove Street. When Anywhere demanded a lawyer, the suits left and signaled the cops to make them talk. Then they came into the observation room, poured themselves a cup of coffee, and watched the unfolding brutality with amusement.

In spite of what they suffered, neither ArgoKnight gave up shit. I had to respect that. Once I crushed the camera like an accordion, I grabbed their cell phones. They looked harmless enough. My psychic touch suggested otherwise. Both cells had well-encrypted call histories, mainly with staff from a vacant building in

Uptown. There was also a picture of my selfie—the one I took on the dead O'Flernan's phone.

Wait.

Deidre O'Flernan was behind this. The bitch had all types of connections, not to mention corrupt officials under her thumb. For example, she could arrange for a pair of dirty Interpol agents to torture Pinpoint and Anywhere. She could also hire (or even buy) a merc firm and expand like crazy. Deidre O'Flernan was after my old market.

When I was done, I'd have to swing by this vacant building and find some answers.

Wondering if this night would ever end, I slipped their phones into my coat. Just as I grabbed the suits' guns, a pair of uniformed cops bravely rushed into the observation room. The first cop got booted in his flabby gut. The second one got knocked off his skinny feet by his fellow officer. I then slammed the door and hopped back into the interrogation room. Along the way, I tossed the guns into Anywhere's lap and sized him up. The teleporter needed a healer, double-quick. Ironically, they put a band-aid on his right arm—probably where they dosed him with Paucium.

My wakizashi came out as I headed over to Pinpoint and flipped her face down.

"Kill me quickly," she sullenly begged through a bloodied mouth.

I deftly sliced through her cuffs without nicking her back. Cops were loudly assembling on the other side of the interrogation room door.

"Get your ass up!" I barked as I stood up and slashed out one of the overhead fluorescent panels.

Glass fell past me as half the room went dark, giving me plenty of shadows. I sheathed the blade while Pinpoint scrambled to her bare feet and spotted the guns in Anywhere's lap. Surprised to be alive, she ran over broken glass and crouched at Anywhere's side. Her good hand grabbed one of the guns from his lap as she eyed him with a lover's concern. I noticed a band-aid on her good arm.

"They dose you too?" I asked with a nod toward the band-aid.

Without turning away from him, Pinpoint angrily emptied the clip at the door. One of her shots missed the door entirely. The rest didn't. I heard two screams of pain from the other side. While the shooter might've been dosed, she was still talented.

"Hang in there, baby," Pinpoint said as she kissed Anywhere's bloodied forehead.

Anywhere and Pinpoint were a couple?!

A year ago, if I had to gauge Pinpoint, I'd have called her the closest thing to perfection. The quick-witted killer was efficient and ruthless. She never hesitated, never second-guessed herself. I've seen Pinpoint kill people (guilty and innocent alike) without a fucking qualm. Throw a crisis her way and she'd come up with a plan within two seconds. That's how she earned my respect—and then my trust.

Now, she had dropped to her knees, grabbed her man, and broke down crying. Anywhere was her Kryptonite. It was sad to watch. It was also annoying that I hadn't figured them out sooner. The sounds of more footsteps approached.

"Shit," I muttered as I created a new shadow portal.

"Follow me," I growled as I shoved her aside.

Anywhere's chair was bolted to the floor. Pinpoint gawked up at me as I ripped it loose—with Anywhere still cuffed to it. He bled on my left shoulder as I carried him through the portal. Scrambling to her feet, Pinpoint grabbed the other gun and followed me through.

"Band-Aid!" I shouted as I hopped out of the shadow portal. "Front and center! I've got a flatline for—"

I stopped and gawked as Pinpoint stumbled out past me. We stood in Meadows Park, practically in the same clearing where I killed those junkies. Their bodies were long-gone, probably taken by other denizens of the park. In a town like this, even corpses had value. That's not what shocked me.

The reception committee threw me off.

Gratte, Gunrack, Forecast, Diglet, Speck, Band-Aid, and Glue were waiting and ready to fight. Standing in a U-shaped formation, they all wore ArgoKnight uniforms, badges, goggles, and utility sashes. Gratte and Gunrack each wielded energy pistols, which were aimed right at me.

"On your knees, Cly," Gratte ordered as he produced Malcolm's Mark-10 inhibitor collar.

CHAPTER SEVENTEEN

"Oh come the fuck on!" I yelled, angrily dumping Anywhere to the ground. "This is bullshit!"

I closed the portal behind me, right as a bunch of cops rushed into the interrogation room.

"Final warning," Gratte ordered.

"You don't even have super powers!" I yelled. "How the fuck are you an ArgoKnight?!"

"Long story, Cly," Gratte replied with a hint of sadness.

"Band-Aid!" Pinpoint shouted as she rushed to her lover's side. "He's flatlined!"

The heroes' eyes turned toward Anywhere.

"His mind's intact—barely," Band-Aid announced as she gave her boss a questioning glance.

"Shit!" Gratte sighed as he reluctantly gave her the nod.

With Band-Aid out of the fight, I had a chance (and they knew it).

"I need two uninterrupted minutes," replied the healer with a worried glance my way.

"Anywhere's got a psi-screen better than most dictators," I pointed out. "Doesn't he have to let you in first?"

"ArgoKnight psi-screens have allowances for this sort of thing," Gunrack explained. "Positive psychic powers, like healing, don't get blocked."

Hmm. Good to know.

I sighed and looked around. Yeah, I could've turned Anywhere's condition to my advantage and fled—or just beaten them down. Instead, I glared over at Pinpoint and gave her the T-sign. She took the hint and tossed her gun with a sigh of relief. Still not believing this bullshit, I walked away from the lovers. Band-Aid cautiously approached Anywhere and knelt beside him.

I went to the picnic table. The heroes watched me, expecting some devious, sneaky attack. Actually, I just wanted a smoke. I plucked a Marlboro.

"Call this a two-minute smoke break," I offered. "Then it'll be eight-on-one and we can kill each other like civilized crime fighters."

Gratte swapped confused glances with the others. Gunrack allowed herself a smile as she came over. My eyes dropped to her hips, which swayed as she approached.

I was going to miss those hips.

"Fine," Gunrack said as she reached the table. "You've earned it."

My ex sat next to me without letting her tension show. I offered Gunrack my pack, which she accepted. The gesture was more of a courtesy.

"So," I asked as I handed her my lighter, "how's Grace?"

"Still comatose from whatever you did to her," Gunrack replied with a hint of praise. "Our psi-docs say that she'll recover in a day or two."

"And her implants?" I asked.

"I think the data's salvageable," Gunrack sighed. "Either way, they'll take me a week to fix."

"Ya' don't say?" I muttered, glad that I had let Reckoner walk. "By the by, have the bad guys breached your lab yet?"

"They tried about thirty minutes ago," Gunrack smirked. "We're questioning the survivors at another location."

I found myself oddly impressed.

"I thought ArgoKnights couldn't be 'ruthless-killer' types."

Gunrack leaned in close.

"Don't tell anyone."

We shared a smile. Gunrack bit her lip and then looked over at me.

"When this is over, we should have a talk . . . about us."

"No need," I replied, as my smile went away. "There is no 'us.' I was just a mission, yeah?"

"Yeah," she lied with saddened eyes. "I wish things were different."

"At least you learned some sex tricks for the next guy," I shrugged, hoping I wouldn't have to kill her ass tomorrow.

Glue cautiously approached with clear suspicion in his eyes. His funky little kinetic weapon was slung over his shoulder.

"Why aren't you dead?" Glue flat-out asked.

"It ain't Irish luck," I muttered.

"What about Grace's instability?" he pressed.

"Handled," came my casual reply.

I realized that they all had questions in their heads—mainly centering on what the fuck happened tonight. Maybe I should tell them everything, in case I died and this night's events were lost to time . . .

Nah. Fuck 'em.

"Where's Malcolm?" Gratte asked.

"Safe," I assured him.

"There's no such word, Cly," he argued. "The kid's safer with us."

I laughed so hard that I almost choked on the smoke. Gratte folded his arms with annoyance as he looked around. None of his colleagues believed him either. By now, they had to know that they had (at least) one traitor amongst them.

"And, um, how many trainees and trainers made it out?" I tried to ask with a straight face.

Silence.

"The response team just got there ten minutes ago," Gratte replied. "So far, nothing but bodies. Thanks for killing those assholes."

"A pleasure," I grinned, taking credit for Reckoner's work.

"That's a curious thing," Gunrack asked as she handed me back my lighter. "Why'd you warn us to stay away?"

"Common courtesy," I replied, thinking of Reckoner and what it would do if Grace's pals had shown up during its rampage.

I reached into my coat and pulled out the two cell phones taken from the precinct.

"These belonged to two dead Brits. They claimed to be Interpol agents," I explained as I slapped them on the table. "They were overseeing Pinpoint's near-rape."

Gratte's shocked eyes turned toward Pinpoint (who confirmed my words with a sullen nod). I took a drag from my cigarette.

"The calls originated from a building in Uptown," I continued. "I was about to go over and level the place when Anywhere up and died on me."

The heroes spared a glance at Anywhere. The teleporter looked just as dead as when I left him. Band-Aid tuned us out as she continued working on him.

"You know who's behind this?" Gratte asked, eager for some payback.

"Not yet," I lied, wondering what Deidre was out to gain. "Once I'm done with you, I'll go have a look."

"What makes you think that you can take the eight of us?" Glue asked.

"Bitch, please!" I laughed. "Your only real threat is Band-Aid. Which reminds me . . ."

I pulled out my pouch of bribe diamonds and tossed them at the healer. She snatched them out of the air without even looking my way.

"Feels like diamonds," Band-Aid smiled. "Street value?"

"A little over two-mil," I replied.

"You shouldn't have," Band-Aid grinned.

"I owe you for giving me my old powers back," I explained. "I'd have died without 'em."

"Band-Aid! Focus!" Pinpoint hissed, gesturing at her lover's body.

The healer tucked the diamonds into her uniform, before resuming her work. That's when I noticed Forecast. The kid was pacing back-and-forth in the distance, just itching to fight. Hoping I wouldn't have to kill her, I leaned back on the table and smoked.

About a minute later, Anywhere abruptly began coughing as his eyes opened. Gratte smiled as Pinpoint wrapped Anywhere up with her good arm. Still handcuffed to the chair, the teleporter's eyes narrowed on me with surprise. Pinpoint followed his gaze and then whispered into his ear, probably bringing him up to speed.

I sat up and stubbed out the cigarette into my right palm.

"Well," I hopped off the table, "thanks for the smoke break."

"We don't have to do this," Gunrack said, stubbing her cigarette against the table. "You're in danger."

"Says who?" I shook my head as I glared at Forecast. "The gal with the fucked-up power?"

"She's never wrong," Gratte insisted.

I pointed to Gunrack's sensor goggles.

"You've scanned me, yes?" I asked.

"Yeah," she frowned.

"And?" I pressed.

"Your mutation's stable," Gunrack admitted.

"Which is why Band-Aid earned herself some diamonds tonight," I said, readying Malcolm's psi-link.

If they made a move, controlling all eight of them would be tricky—but doable.

"Before I drop you bitches," I continued, "I've gotta ask: what the fuck is this God-horrible vision anyway?!"

Anywhere teleported out of his handcuffs and slowly stood up. Pinpoint picked up her gun. Band-Aid didn't have to move. The other ArgoKnights readied their powers, weapons, and gadgets.

"You were infected by spores," Forecast explained, as her right hand drifted toward her badge. "When you died last year, they mutated you. Originally, ACHE halted the mutation and stabilized it."

"Yeah. And?" I impatiently pressed.

"Sometime tonight," she continued, "your mutation becomes an airborne virus. You become Patient Zero. The vision had you standing in this park—right here—surrounded by corpses . . . one of them mine. I was in an ArgoKnight uniform. This one, in fact."

That did sound bad. Still, I didn't buy Forecast's argument. Biting my tongue, I simply folded my arms and let her continue.

"The second you wrecked my armor, I knew the outcome couldn't be changed," Forecast explained. "You had just finished feeding on our minds . . . and our corpses were starting to turn into shadowpaths."

"Who else did I infect?" I asked a bit bothered by the idea.

"A bunch of local thugs out for a thrill."

I wonder if she was referring to the junkies I dealt with earlier.

"Well kid, that's not gonna happen," I sighed, feeling a bit sorry for her. "We've changed the future so much—"

"It will happen!" Forecast shouted as spittle flew from her mouth. "Every night I see it in my dreams!

You're going to turn and *nothing* we have done so far has changed that!"

She noticed our concerned stares. I could tell we were all wondering the same thing: had Forecast lost her fucking mind?

"I'm never wrong," she reminded them. "Imagine that kind of plague in a city of millions!"

Pillar City overrun by infectious shadow mutations? That was cringe-worthy.

"Please, Dad," she pleaded. "Stand down."

I sighed and looked them over. The heroes stood poised to fight. If she was right, my decision could affect billions.

The logical thing would be to . . .

"Nice try," I smirked.

Forecast threw her hands up with frustration.

Gratte decided to step in. "Cly, her vision's real! We've had it picked over by our telepaths."

"Can't you see that she's fucking playing you?!" I asked.

"Easy, Cly!" Gunrack interjected. "Can't you tell she's scared?"

"She's playing you!" I snapped as I turned and pointed at Forecast. "I can also tell that someone's monkeyed around with her fucking mind!"

Forecast shook her head, deeply in denial.

"Think, people!" I shouted. "If I were going to become a fucking monster, the logical thing to do would be to—I don't know—fucking warn me! Like, months ago! If Gunrack can sweet-talk me into handcuffs, she could damn-sure convince me of this!"

That made them pause.

"Fuck your old beefs with me," I sneered. "You needed me out there, saving the world. Only thing was I would never become an ArgoKnight. Thus, you poisoned me with a chemical leash. Even without

Forecast's visions, you'd have done it . . . just in case I
went rogue."

I glanced over at Gunrack, who looked down with a
hint of admissive guilt.

"But never fear!" I mocked. "You can replace me,
right? Maybe with someone I helped train, who can
smell danger and face it with state-of-art battle armor?"

Gratte's pokerface melted a bit as he glanced over
at Forecast. Yeah. She was their Plan B.

"Of course, if she betrayed me then she'll betray
you," I reasoned. "It's all part of someone else's puppet
show . . . and none of you see the strings."

Speck and Diglet appeared half-convinced, as did
Pinpoint and Gunrack. The others weren't quite sold.

"Why won't anyone listen to me?" Forecast
sobbingly asked, still shaking her head. "Why won't
anyone listen?!"

"Calm down, Forecast," Gunrack said. "We believe
you."

"No you don't!" Forecast snapped in reply. "But
that's all right."

My kid tapped her badge with an eerie little smile.
"I'll stop him."

A translucent forcefield formed around her. Under
the park's lighting, Forecast's features were partially
obscured as she slipped into a fighting stance.

"What the hell?!" Gunrack gawked, just as shocked
as I was.

Apparently, the badge gadget wasn't one of her
designs.

"He has to be stopped!" Forecast yelled as she
rushed in with a wild punch.

I blocked it and the flurry of punches that followed.
Whoever was mucking around with Forecast's head had
outfitted her with tech to boot. She sent a right
roundhouse kick at my face. I ducked—just as she

pirouetted around and planted a right uppercut into my gut.

I went flying over the picnic table and slammed into a tree. Thanks to my costume, it didn't hurt so much. I looked up just as she came barreling my way again. I had to be careful. That badge's forcefield was equivalent to a suit of high-tech battle armor. Odds were that it had other nifty features as well.

Not in the mood to play defense, I blocked another high roundhouse kick and then tackled her. As we hit the grass, she was already twisting out from under me. Forecast managed to roll on top and started landing punches. Her hits to my unprotected face hurt, so I threw her off. Forecast rolled to her feet while I put my damned mask back on.

"Forecast!" Gratte yelled. "Stand down!"

Forecast ignored the order and rushed in as I started to rise. I grabbed her wrists. She slipped both of them free and then head-butted me in the face. Down I went, with her on top.

"I've got to stop him!" she screamed while trying to strangle me in a two-handed front choke.

I slipped the hold and tried to put her in a guillotine choke . . . to no avail. The others gathered around as we grappled on the grass. The kid was using everything I had taught her and then some. The forcefield made Forecast an honest-to-God threat. Her evasions, strikes, and grapples were all top-level moves.

I should've been physically superior. Instead, her armor leveled the playing field. After several seconds of intense wrestling, Forecast managed to kick me off her. I got knocked a few feet away, rolled, and ended up on my feet. Forecast snarled as she stood up, ready for more.

"Subdue her," Gratte ordered.

With a cry of rage, Forecast started to move toward me—only to find her feet stuck to the grass, courtesy of Glue's adhesion field. Diglet ran in and pounded her armor with a few hundred strikes per second.
Unhindered by the adhesion field, the speedster danced around her at normal speed, while his hands moved too fast for my eye to follow. Forecast covered her face as her armor rippled from Diglet's punches. I could tell he was pulling his strikes, which were intended to distract instead of harm.

Forecast reached for her utility sash. As it was underneath her forcefield, Diglet couldn't get to it. He tried to grab her right hand and muscle her down, which was his mistake. Forecast swatted the speedster away with a right backhand across his torso. While his uniform took the brunt of the impact, Diglet slammed into Glue. As both supers hit the grass, Glue lost his concentration.

Free to move, Forecast rushed toward me. Gunrack raised her pistols and fired. Wads of something whizzed past Forecast, who nimbly somersaulted over the incoming projectiles. In mid-evasion, the kid squeezed a marble bomb and threw it at me. I couldn't dodge the explosive, which bounced off my chest and fell to the grass.

"Grenade!" Speck yelled as she came out of nowhere and dove on the fucking thing.

Shit!

Even Forecast's eyes went wide. She only wanted to fuck me up—not Speck. Unable to do anything, we all watched the marble bomb explode . . . with a muffled pop? Ah. Speck shrank it. Instead of getting blown to tiny bits, the shrinker rolled onto her back with a pained groan. The blast didn't even scorch her uniform.

"Nice save," I said with a relieved smile.

"I'm too old for this shit," Speck griped.

"Not in my opinion," I grinned as I hopped over her and ran toward Forecast.

Eyes still on me, the kid plucked another item from her gadget belt. Just before Forecast could throw it, Pinpoint opened fire. Her perfect shot caused a red disc to explode in my daughter's hand! The blast enveloped Forecast in a red, acidic mist. Horrified, I jumped back.

"Damn it!" Pinpoint hissed.

Acid bombs were standard ArgoKnight gear, used primarily to deal with metallic barriers and/or threats (like hostile drones). It was against the rules to use one against a living target, which meant that Forecast had truly gone psycho. Seeing as the mist could melt through titanium in seconds, we figured she was done for.

Instead, she emerged from the acid cloud without injury. The ground around her was scorched with the high-intensity corrosive. While her acid-soaked forcefield was smoking, it looked to be intact. Worse, she leaped into the night air with the clear intention of acid wrestling with me. Still on his back, Glue shot her out of the air with his kinetic blaster. Forecast flew sideways, hit the ground, and then came up with a perfect roll.

Her forcefield was still dripping acid as she stood up.

Gunrack's pistols tagged her and the wads exploded on impact. They formed a gray mist and then solidified into something resembling hardened concrete. Whatever it was engulfed Forecast in a head-to-toe cocoon. Unable to break free, Forecast squirmed underneath. The audible hissing of acid implied that the restraint wouldn't hold. Worse, if Forecast could get the right gadget(s) out, the kid might blast free (and die in the process).

"Can she breathe in that?" I asked.

"Yeah," Gunrack worriedly replied. "What the fuck's wrong with her?"

"We need to get a team of telepaths in her head," Gratte concluded as he pulled a radio. "Someone's done a number on her mind."

"Gee, ya' think?!" I snapped. "Just keep her contained. I got this."

I kicked on the psi-link, telepathy, and memory powers. Then I reclined on my back and tried to focus.

"What are you gonna do?" Pinpoint asked as she stepped up to my right.

"Something really, really stupid," I replied. "Watch my back and have Band-Aid check Forecast's vitals. Depending on what's in her head, things might get dicey."

"Wait," Gunrack balked, "you're trusting us? After everything we've done to you?"

I glanced over at Anywhere, who had calmly picked up the Mark-10 collar. He thoughtfully twirled it in his right hand as he met my gaze.

"I don't trust you," I told him. "I trust in your sense of self-preservation."

"What does that mean?" Gratte asked, clearly weighing his options.

I glared up at my former friend.

"I'm going to go save my daughter now," I explained. "If anything disrupts my efforts, anything at all, you fucks better die trying to stop it. 'Cause if I lose her, you're all dead: painfully, thoroughly, and without a shred of mercy. Once I'm done with you, I will personally kill every surviving ArgoKnight. Please believe that."

Gratte considered my threat for a moment. Then he regarded Forecast. Still trapped in the cocoon, we could all hear her raging struggle to escape.

"Overwatch positions," he sighed. "Band-Aid, sedate her."

Band-Aid nodded and looked over at Forecast for a moment, then frowned with surprise.

"Her mind's blocked," she reported. "I think it's the forcefield."

The other ArgoKnights spread out to form a defensive perimeter around Forecast and me. I tuned out my surroundings. Having done this shit twice already, my head was fatigued in so many ways. Frankly, I was in no condition to work on Lia's psyche. It was stronger than mine. Worse, she might have guests in her skull.

Anyone else, I'd have considered resting up and then going in. But this was my kid . . . and she needed me.

Still, between the stolen mind powers, I had a chance to save her. Her ArgoKnight psi-screen wouldn't stop me because my intentions were benign. The Omega-level psi-link could punch through anything (even her armor). If I could find the point of psychic manipulation, maybe I could "edit" it away. Of course, one little mistake and her mind could be ruined. The realization made me hesitate for a moment.

Then I took a deep breath and plunged into Lia's mind.

CHAPTER EIGHTEEN

Thanks to Malcolm's psi-link, I was able to slice past Lia's forcefield and formidable will with ease. Deeper and deeper I went . . . until I slammed into a sandy beach with enough force to create a small crater. Pain lanced through my upper body as sand fell all around. The cold sky was cloudy enough to keep the shadows to a minimum.

With a groan, I cut the psi-link. Leaving it up was just too risky.

If someone (or something) lurked in her mind, it could easily rip control of the psi-link from my tired mind. Hopefully, someone had simply altered her mind from afar. Back in the day, my telepaths would brainwash someone, leave a few psychic triggers behind, and call it day. Without the psi-link, maybe I could use the SWAP cop's powers and undo the psi-manipulation.

Of course, severing the psi-link was fucking suicidal.

Psychic Combat 101 had one simple rule: never get into a psi-fight without a psychic anchor. Every psychic attack and/or manipulation that I've done tonight has been from inside of my own body (psychic anchor). The psi-link could also be counted as a psychic anchor. Without either of these, I was essentially feeding on my own mind.

The longer I stayed in Forecast's head, the weaker I'd get. My guess was that I'd last a few minutes before my psyche fell apart. Once the purge was finished, I could reactivate the psi-link and climb the fuck out.

My crazy little plan might've worked . . . had my stolen powers not decided to blink out right then and there. Why? I had no idea. Without those powers (especially Malcolm's psi-link), this became a one-way

187 · Murder Sauce

trip. Granted, I had my weapons and core abilities. Too bad they wouldn't amount to much in here.

I heard Lia's laughter as I spat out some sand and achingly looked up. Crouched nearby, she was apparently unharmed and . . . maybe twenty years older. Her dyed-blonde hair was tied up in thick, long locks, which draped around her face and ran down her back. Lia looked just like her late mother, except her dark-green eyes were both wiser and hardened with a history of mayhem.

Her costume was a step up as well.

Black-and-green, the lightweight body armor looked metallic and had been tailored for her tall frame. She had picked up some muscle tone, along with a bunch of weapons and gadgetry. Her personal arsenal included a pair of large-caliber machine pistols and a wakizashi that looked a lot like mine. She wore the scabbarded blade across the small of her back.

Designed without any logos, the armor even came with a hooded black cape that fluttered in the coastal breeze.

"Still as graceful as I remember," Lia giggled.

Even her voice and speech patterns were different, more mature.

"What's so funny?" I asked as I used the power gaze on her.

To my surprise, I realized that this wasn't some possessive entity or a telepath's mind game. This was Lia—broken precog and all.

"Just the fact that you die trying to save me," Lia replied as her hands drifted toward her hip-holstered sidearms.

"How's that funny?" I groaned.

Her expression fell.

"I see your point," Lia replied. "Sorry about the fall."

"I'll live," I said as I stepped toward her.

"Not for much longer."

She was right. My strength was ebbing.

"The sad part's that you haven't put two-and-two together yet," Lia sighed. "I remembered you being smarter than this."

"Enlighten me," I replied, ready for whatever came my way.

"First off, no one's pulling my strings," she sneered. "No evil mastermind's whispering into my ear. I did most of this. *Me.*"

Well . . . that changed things.

"My evil, diabolical plan's to put you in the ground; along with every remaining ArgoKnight," Lia replied with a pearly-white smile that was less than sane.

I took a deep breath and looked for any decent options. Too bad there weren't any. At this point, I could fight or talk. Lia would have the edge in a fight—and she knew it. Odds were that her mind was (somehow) booby trapped against intrusion. It would explain how the extra powers fell away from me.

Lia could outlast me in hand-to-hand. Weapon-to-weapon, it could go either way. If I could talk her down . . . nah. I could already tell that she was too far-gone. Still, Lia was my kid. I had to try.

Eyes on her, I fished out my Marlboros and pulled one with my teeth. She fondly eyed me as I turned my back to the wind and lit up.

"Want one?" I asked. "You're legal."

"Sure," she replied with a cocky smile.

I tossed my daughter the pack. She caught it and gestured for the lighter, which I also tossed.

"Clever, Dad," Lia grinned as she cupped her hands against the wind and lit up. "Everyone always thought you were a compulsive smoker. In reality, you only took one when you needed to stall for time or think something through."

"True," I admitted. "Of course, I sometimes smoked for the mere fuck of it."

She dropped my smokes and lighter to the sand. As casual as Lia seemed, I knew she was quietly daring me to make the first move.

"Ask your questions," Lia told me with utter confidence, "When I flick the butt away, you die."

I eyed the cloudy sky for a sad moment.

"My little girl's dead, isn't she?" I asked.

She nodded.

"You appear to be a grown-up version of Lia, though," I frowned. "How?"

"I'll tell you at the end of our little timeout," she replied. "If it's any consolation, I'm a lot more suited for what comes next."

"And that is?"

"Some truly dark times," Lia earnestly replied. "For example, you're supposed to die tonight. That's when the kill team burst into your loft."

"Really?" I snickered as I folded my arms. "You saw that in a vision, didja'?"

Lia shook her head.

"To me, it was history," she replied. "For one thing, you never ran into Wabbit."

I grinned. "What really happened then?"

"The same merc firm that hit the ArgoKnights hit us," Lia replied with evident anger on her face. "They wanted both of us alive."

Damn. That made sense. Maybe her trip into the past had changed my future as well.

"When they breached, their inhibitor pulse ruined my armor," Lia explained before giving me a proud smile. "Even without your powers, you killed half of them. I barely got out in the crossfire. By the time it was over, most of your building was blown to pieces."

"Then what?"

Lia exhaled smoke through her nose as a host of bad memories crossed her face.

"I buried you," she quietly explained. "The surviving ArgoKnights went after *Status Quo*, the merc assholes who killed you."

"How'd that turn out?" I asked.

"Messy. We were outnumbered and outclassed," Lia continued. "Still, we managed to take them out. Hell, I might've remained an ArgoKnight . . . before I found out about the chemical leash. After that, I killed them too."

The hateful look on Lia's face made me believe her. Then it hit me.

"Wait . . . you're saying that they'd have poisoned me? Even without your bullshit vision?!"

She nodded.

"Even though you were their ace world-saver, the ArgoKnights were terrified of you," Lia explained. "Popping through shadows, drinking minds, and flat-out kicking ass throughout the world."

My daughter gave me a sentimental smile.

"You were a legend, Dad. Twenty years after your death, people were still speaking of you in frightened whispers."

"And ACHE's genetic therapy—that was your idea?"

"Mm-hm," she grinned. "Harlot kept constant tabs on your activities, so she knew that your powers were watered down. When she finally had an excuse to take you out, she sent one of her lesser teams to bring you in alive. That's why you came out on top."

"Why'd you sic that bitch on me?" I asked.

Lia's expression shifted to one of mild guilt. "A small part of me was hoping you'd run. But you never run, do you?"

I wanted to kick the shit out of my kid right now. Instead, I took a drag of my cigarette and controlled my anger. There were too many questions to ask and no time to fucking ask them!

"Who gave that bitch the layout of my place?" I asked, bothered that I hadn't figured that part out yet.

"Lou," Lia matter-of-factly replied. "Harlot threatened his family, so . . ."

That's how I'd beat her.

Part of Lou's augmentation came with a string of psychic failsafes that he didn't know about. Should he ever betray me, his subconscious mind would actually make him screw up. That's why he forgot to warn Harlot's team to call me "Mr. Cly" when they tried to steer me to the rooftop.

Also, should Lou ever try to kill me (and I knowingly let him), the failsafe would shut his brain off before he could attempt the deed. All of my security guys had the same safeties built into their augmentations because I used to be paranoid. Then along came Gunrack. Love had made me sloppy.

The thing was, Lia had similar protections in her mind.

Teke slipped them in back when she was learning how to control her precog abilities. As a fixer, my cold rationale was that someone could flip this innocent kid against me. If that day ever came, the failsafe would ensure that Lia screwed up.

As with Lou, if I let her try to kill me, she'd simply die. That was my slim chance. Of course, I was assuming that Lia hadn't disarmed her own mind. If she had, letting her kill me was akin to suicide. Worse, in order to win this little standoff, all the kid had to do now was wait for me to die.

"Band-Aid didn't restore my augmentations," I suddenly realized. "You did."

"That's the Cly I remember," Lia winked. "I countered their chemical leash with a mutagenic compound. It gets invented about ten years from now."

"You meant for me to get my old powers back?"

"Yes and no," Lia replied with a shrug. "I wanted your monster self to come back. Only, Band-Aid had to go and twist your mutation. I must admit; kickstarting your old augments was a fucking stroke of genius on her part."

"Then why'd she do it?" I asked. "Band-Aid's an ArgoKnight. Curing me of the chemical leash made no sense."

"It does if she's also a well-paid mole for the Povchenko mob," Lia chuckled.

I exhaled deeply at that news. If she was really a Russian mole, then the Povchenkos knew everything about the ArgoKnights, *Lairs 'R Us*, and (possibly) me.

"When she told the Russians about the chemical leash, they instructed her to both cure and warn you."

I puffed my cigarette for a thoughtful second or two.

"Ah," I realized, "they wanted me to flip out and start killing ArgoKnights."

"I'd have been cool with that," Lia nodded with a scary gleam in her eye.

"Sorry I didn't follow through," I smirked.

"Well, we did give you every excuse," she admitted. "Too bad you're such a gentleman."

We both chuckled at that last part. I could barely stand. Another minute and I'd be on my back.

"You could've ratted her out," I noted. "Why didn't you?"

"Connor O'Flernan and his fucking kid," Lia replied with a roll of her eyes. "When I heard that you saved them, I was so tempted to kill Malcolm right then and there."

Seeing as she dosed the kid, it could've been easy for her to "arrange" an accident of some kind.

"What happened in the original timeline?" I asked.

"Glue and Nolan get killed. Deidre captures the kid and grooms him as her protégé."

"Then something changed," I frowned. "In this timeline, the O'Flernan shooters were out to kill Malcolm."

Lia gave me a mischievous grin.

"Someone might've tipped Deidre off about the thing in Malcolm's head."

If I were Deidre, I'd kill the kid too. That much power, while tempting, was too dangerous. Not to mention uncontrollable.

"In the original timeline," she continued, "no one else knew about Connor. He only came out whenever his son was in danger. About six years later, Deidre dies. Through Malcolm, Connor takes over the O'Flernan mob and starts a war with the other mobs."

"Who won?" I asked.

"Malcolm almost had it sewn up," she replied. "Then I came along and killed them both . . . which wasn't easy. I figured that, with Band-Aid's upgrades, you'd do the same and save me the trouble."

Lia and I smoked in silence as my legs trembled from the effort of keeping me vertical. I had to think of something. Some way to avoid what was coming . . .

"You set up the attack on the training center," I guessed.

"Nope," Lia replied. "The ArgoKnights' secret resurgence was blown from day one."

"They fucked it up that badly?" I asked with a shaky voice.

"Yeah," Lia nodded with raised eyebrows. "My God, Dad! They didn't last a year!"

"Where'd they go wrong?" I pressed, genuinely curious.

Lia walked over to me and came within striking distance. As tempted as I was to rip her (or try to), I decided to play nice; to trust her one last time. She gently tapped my chest with her right palm. The gesture was a soft psychic contact, through which some of her memories flowed.

I frowned at what I saw.

The three ArgoKnight Section Chiefs were Grace, Gratte, and Gunrack. Entrusted with restoring the ArgoKnights, they were killed within days of my death. Lia knew of (at least) nine other moles in the newly reformed ArgoKnights (all representing different interests). A bunch of old-school ArgoKnights stupidly came out of hiding . . . and were slaughtered for their loyalty. Their methods and safe houses were compromised to the point where one could find them on Google!

Through her eyes, I saw the bloody fight between the ArgoKnights and *Status Quo*. Then I watched her kill most of the heroes who survived—even Band-Aid. Other interested parties picked off the ones she missed. By next spring, the final ArgoKnight was confirmed dead.

"How'd you walk away from that?" I asked.

"I went underground," Lia replied with a hint of pride. "Thanks to my training and powers, I managed to stay ahead of your enemies . . . and made new ones of my own. Eventually, I decided to sell my talents."

"As what? A spy?" I asked, knowing I was wrong.

"No, Dad," Lia shook her head and tapped her chest armor. There was a flash of white holographic light as the word *Murder Sauce* appeared in vertical Japanese text.

"I ended up in the family business," she smugly confessed.

I frowned.

"You became a fixer?!"

Lia nodded.

"That's the name of your firm? *Murder Sauce?*"

She nodded. "I worked out of Tokyo. Before I came back here, I had 301 high-end mercs on my payroll."

Part of me was impressed. The rest was saddened. I don't know what I would've expected Lia to become. A do-gooder, perhaps. Maybe some sort of protector. In spite of her lethal, hard-nosed training, the kid had a heart of gold. Then the world had torn all of the goodness out of her, leaving this twisted bitch in its wake.

Forecast.

"No regrets, Dad," she assured me. "If you had raised me soft, I'd have ended up dead or someone's mind toy."

Our cigarettes were almost gone.

For some reason, Forecast decided to walk down this bloody path. She wanted/needed me dead and I didn't know why. I fell on my ass. Her stance shifted as I went down, ready to attack or defend. Then my daughter looked around with a knowing smile.

"Bad move, severing the psi-link," she teased. "If you had left it up, you might've won."

"Tell me about how you got here," I said, ignoring the fact that I couldn't feel my legs.

The fixer's eyes watched me with cold anticipation.

"My younger self had her last vision about six months back; just after you broke her power," Forecast explained. "Unable to control it, her mind jumped twenty-five years into the future. I believe the date was April 6th, 2038."

A hint of regret flashed across her face.

"The strain was too much," she explained.

"Why?" I asked.

Forecast gave me a look of mild pity. "You remember how her visions used to work, Dad. They didn't show you the future . . . they actually took you there."

I nodded, remembering how realistic her visions were. Lia could only do it once per day and it always hurt. Her will was too strong for psi-training. What I originally saw as irritating limitations were really safeguards that kept her both alive and sane.

"Even though I have much greater control, my visions still hurt," Forecast admitted. "The further I look into the future (or the past), the greater the psychic toll. My younger self simply went too far into the future and her mind couldn't cope."

My eyes began to water.

"This was my fault," I said with a trembling voice. "If I hadn't broken her power . . ."

"She'd have died anyway—along with everyone in Pillar City," argued Forecast.

That cold truth didn't comfort me one fucking bit.

"I felt her mind touch mine," the fixer softly explained. "As she died, her power dragged me across time like a fucking yo-yo."

Tears rolled down my face. I wiped them away.

"I . . . I didn't know that was possible," I said.

"Me neither," Forecast admitted. "Next thing I knew, I woke up in my old bed and I'm twenty-five years younger."

"Why didn't you tell me?" I asked, feeling betrayed (again).

"I realized that I needed to seed my future," Forecast explained. "I needed resources, contacts, and a safe haven. Besides, you might've killed me."

Forecast had some valid points. I feebly raised the cigarette to my lips. Forecast flicked hers into the wind, ready for anything.

"Speaking to that," I asked. "Why make me out to be a threat to humanity?"

Forecast gave me a casual shrug. In that moment, I caught a glimpse of her well-concealed madness.

"It was a goofy plan but it worked, yeah?" she explained. "As for my visions, I gave the ArgoKnights perfect intel and earned their trust. Then I faked a vision about you."

"Good enough to fool their telepaths?" I frowned.

"Faking memories is just one of my many tricks, Dad," she replied.

"Why take me down at all?" I asked again. "I wasn't your enemy."

Forecast searched for the right explanation.

"You're the only one who can stop me," came her ominous reply.

"That's not true," I shrugged, "Gratte's team managed to stuff you in a cocoon easily enough."

"Riiiight," Forecast scoffed. "That fight in the park was just pretend. I wanted you to jump into my mind and you took the bait. Once you're dead, I'll kill your pals."

"If you say so," I shrugged, fairly certain that it wouldn't be that simple.

Forecast didn't look bothered. "My costume's loaded with custom gadgets that I've made myself. I could negate their powers with the press of a button."

"You make gadgets too?" I frowned.

Forecast indifferently shrugged. "Psi-training psychics gets easier (and safer) in the future. Once I got here, all I had to do was draw up the specs and swap them with some inventors I met online. In return, they supplied me with working prototypes."

"Impressive," I nodded. "Once I'm dead, then what? You open up shop as a fixer?"

"Something much more difficult," Forecast replied with a cryptic grin, full of murderous possibilities.

"You don't have to do this," I pleaded.

Unable to sit up, I slumped onto my back and stared up at her.

"Actually, Dad, I do."

Forecast reverently pulled the armored hood over her head. Green metal slid from the fabric, somewhat like a red-horned kabuki mask. Probably nanite-based, the armor wrapped around her face and even her dreadlocks.

I looked up at the monster my little girl had become. Forecast knelt beside me and gently pulled the cigarette from my mouth. This was about the craziest gamble I've ever taken. At some point, Forecast might've found (and disabled) Teke's failsafes. Or maybe all of her psychic upgrades rendered them moot.

Either way, I had to let Forecast try to kill me and trust in Teke's work.

"Any chance of you rolling with me?" I offered, knowing she'd refuse. "Whatever it is you're up to, we could go after it together. We could stay a family."

To my surprise, the assassin gave it a few moments of thought. Then she slowly drew her blade.

"Sorry, Dad," Forecast regretfully replied. "I've got ambitions that you just wouldn't approve of—like harvesting your organs."

She curiously cocked her head as I weakly laughed.

"I guess you wanted to be me after all!"

If she could take my abilities, without ruining her intuitive powers, Forecast would be a walking nightmare. It was a worthy ambition—one that couldn't be allowed to happen. I let myself feel the sand and the cold wind.

"Are you ready?" she asked.

I nodded. "Make it quick, huh?"

She paused and studied me for a moment.

"What?" I asked. "Change your mind?"

"No," came her reply. "I was expecting more of a fight from you."

I shook my head.

"I'd lose," I admitted. "We both know that."

"That's never stopped you before," Forecast replied as she expertly placed the tip of her wakizashi against my chest, just over my heart.

"That my blade?" I frowned.

Her balance was perfect. Even now, Forecast was expecting me to make a countermove. Sadly, I wouldn't have to.

"I retrieved it after you died," she explained. "Guess I'll have to steal it again."

I could save her.

Just warn her about the failsafe. She'd let me die and could (probably) kill Gratte and the others. But then what? How many people would she kill along the way? She'd make Teke undo the failsafe (then kill him). Aside from the people I knew, there were the ones she'd have to feed upon—once she became a hungry shadowpath.

There was no other way. My Lia was already dead. This was just another amoral lunatic who needed to be put down.

"Well," I smiled. "It's been a sad pleasure meeting you, Forecast. I . . . I'm sorry I failed you."

"Nonsense," she gently replied. "You'll make me perfect."

Forecast raised the fighting blade over her head with both hands. In spite of her words, one thing was bitterly clear: she wanted this. God help me, she really wanted this.

"To be honest, I couldn't be more grateful," she intimated.

"That's why I'm sorry," I sighed. "Good-bye, kid."

"Good-bye, Dad."

With that, she stabbed downward.

The failsafe kicked in during her strike and her body suddenly spasmed backwards. There was a soft, defiant groan from behind her mask . . . and then she died. The blade fell from her lifeless hands and buried itself in the sand, just above my head. My daughter's corpse slumped across me. I grabbed her and held her close as I screamed the last of my strength away.

In another second or two, I'd join her.

CHAPTER NINETEEN

"Get . . . back . . . here!" A familiar voice growled in my mind.

My eyes snapped open as sharp agony shot through my skull and made me writhe. Able to scream, I did so. It took me a moment or two to get a handle on the pain. Then I noticed labored breathing behind me.

"That wasn't so hard, now was it?" Band-Aid joked.

Relieved not to have an inhibitor collar around my neck, I rolled over and smiled up at the sweaty-faced healer. Then I looked around and realized that everyone else was sprawled out on the grass. Their eyes were open and they appeared to be conscious. They just weren't moving. When I tried to sit up, I realized that I couldn't move either.

"So you're a mole, eh?" I sighed, remembering my chat with Forecast.

"One of many, I suspect," Band-Aid replied as she willed my pain away.

Too bad I still couldn't move.

"Why didn't you just let me die?"

"Well, it had nothing to do with the diamonds you just gave me," she casually replied.

I had to smile at that until I looked over at Lia's cocoon.

"Can you save her?" I asked.

If Band-Aid could save her, Teke might—might—be able to fix her fucked-up mind.

The healer shook her head.

"That forcefield of hers is still up," Band-Aid replied. "I'm sorry."

I fought back tears as I stared up at the fake sky.

"What happens now?" I asked.

Band-Aid looked around at her fellow ArgoKnights and then at my watch.

"The Povchenkos are on their way," Band-Aid tensely explained.

"They'll torture and kill your friends," I pointed out, bothered that I had to stand up for the fuckers. "Is that what you really want?"

"It doesn't matter and you know it," the healer shot back. "They were dead the moment they tried to put the ArgoKnights back together. At least this way I don't die too. The Povchenkos will have my back—especially when I give them Gratte."

"What makes him so special?" I asked.

She gave me a wry grin. "He's ACHE's new host."

That made Gratte *very* valuable—and fucking stupid. From what little Grace had told me about ACHE, the damned thing was like an AI genie to its host. During its stint in my body, it was a fountain of information. ACHE could tell me any mundane fact: from the weather in France to Cleopatra's cup size.

However, I never had full access to its sensitive systems or any ArgoKnight archive files. Then again, neither did Section Chief Gratte. The Outfitter (paranoid genius that he was) only entrusted Grace with junior admin access—but no one else. In my opinion, the dead inventor predicted *Clean Sweep* and designed ACHE to help the survivors regroup. It was plugged into every ArgoKnight base (active or not) and had sixty-nine years worth of their data files.

If the Povchenkos hacked the AI . . .

I gave Band-Aid a low whistle and an appraising nod. She smiled, seeing that I understood her rationale. Sooner or later, someone would've pinned down ACHE's host and compromised the AI. Why shouldn't she do it and earn a fat reward for it?

"They'll love you for that, Band-Aid," I said as I grinned over at Gratte.

The fucker looked up at the healer with helplessness, anger, and terror all over his reddened face.

"I'm glad you understand," Band-Aid replied.

"I do," I politely nodded. "Yet, I can't quite see you as a Russian mobster."

"Me neither," she admitted. "It still beats dying."

"Why'd you become an ArgoKnight, anyway?"

"You could say I was born into it," Band-Aid replied with a hint of spite.

"Ah," I ruefully smiled, remembering my early days in the orphanage. "I know how that can be."

Band-Aid leaned over me and looked me in the eye. I could feel her warm breath on my face as the healer decided my fate.

"I'll let you walk," she offered, "as long as you fuck off and never bother me about this."

After what the ArgoKnights had put me through, it was tempting to leave them twisting in the wind. Very tempting.

"This is just business. No retaliations or any hard feelings. Just accept the fact that the ArgoKnights are a lost cause," Band-Aid proposed. "Can you do that?"

As she could read my every nerve and cranny, the healer was something of a lie detector. Of course, lying wasn't (often) my thing. I honored my deals, which was the main reason she even considered making this one.

"Why are you really letting me go?"

"Seeing as you keep saving the world, you get a pass," she shrugged. "I'll even let you take Forecast with you—out of respect for the dead."

I glanced over at my cocooned daughter's body, bothered that I'd have to cremate her, ASAP. Once word got out that the precog was dead, folks would come after her. After all, Lia's DNA was worth billions in certain circles.

"Deal," I sincerely replied.

Relieved that Lia wouldn't end up on a Povchenko cloning lab, I suddenly found myself able to move. Still on my back, I quickly took off my gloves and gazed myself over. I breathed a sigh of relief. My shadow mutation, power rip, and power gazing abilities were still intact.

"How much time do we have?" I asked as I put my gloves back on. "Before the Russians show?"

"Ten minutes or so," Band-Aid replied. "Why?"

I pulled Gunrack's engagement ring out of my coat and tossed it to her. The healer caught the ring and eyed it under the streetlight. Her eyes widened as I stood up.

"That's for saving me—again," I grimly replied. "Now come on. It's my turn to save you."

I walked over to Anywhere and lightly stepped on his chest. Doing so allowed me to rip his power.

"What are you talking about?" Band-Aid frowned as she pocketed the emerald ring.

"Do you really think your fine black ass won't end up on a lab table?" I scoffed as I stepped on Speck's right shin and ripped her power. "The Povchenkos are about trust and respect. You've just sold out your own people. They're also an insular mob that's 100% Russian. You don't look Russian to me. See how this ends?"

"I'd be a street soldier," Band-Aid shook her head, bothered by my logic. "That's better than being an ArgoKnight with a tag on my toe. My powers make me valuable!"

"No, dear. ACHE *made* you valuable," I reminded her. "Once you hand that over, they'll kill you, sell you to the Colombians, or (if you're lucky) turn you into a brainwashed minion."

She could tell I wasn't lying, which scared her more than my words. I've worked with the Russians long enough to know I was right about this.

"What other choice do I have?!" Band-Aid balked. "The ArgoKnights are dead and done. If I cross the Russians, so am I!"

She had a point there. I stepped on Diglet's chest and ripped him. Then I headed for Glue.

"What are you doing?" Band-Aid asked.

"Going back to work," I muttered. "I'm a crime fighter, remember?"

Band-Aid's eyes suspiciously narrowed.

"You're up to something."

"Band-Aid, you'll kill me if I even twitch wrong," I scoffed. "Besides, I gave you my word."

I stepped on Glue and ripped his power.

"You're on my good side," I sighed, "which is why I'm offering you a third choice. Now get the fuck over here."

The ArgoKnights were just within teleportation range. I could take us well out of the healer's range before she could do shit . . . but I gave her my word.

"They'll kill me, Cly!" Band-Aid hissed.

The traitor was fucking terrified and had every right to be. I took a deep breath.

"I just saved the world from exploding tonight," I told her. "Could I have stopped Connor O'Flernan on my own?"

The healer paused, realizing that I couldn't have.

"These pricks deserve to die," I chuckled. "Yet, I'd be dead without them. Period. So would you and everyone else."

I gestured toward the downed ArgoKnights and then at her.

"Hell! You've saved my life twice already," I reminded her. "You ArgoKnights have your many flaws

. . . but also a few virtues. The most endearing one is that you're stupid enough to fight the good fight. People like them (and you) can still be useful."

Band-Aid started to argue but I raised a hand.

"Fuck the Russians, Band-Aid," I continued. "The cold truth is that the next asshole who wants to wipe out the world will probably win—unless we get in the way."

"They don't have a future!" Band-Aid yelled, noticeably shaking. Tears of fear (and maybe guilt) started down her cheeks as she pointed at the downed heroes. "Over a thousand of us have died, Cly! Friends of mine! Family! They'll hunt us down until every last ArgoKnight is dead!"

"You're right," I sighed. "Doesn't change a thing, though."

The exasperated healer then pointed at Forecast's body.

"I don't get it, Cly!" Band-Aid sobbed. "After all they've taken from you, why would you even think of trying to save them?!"

I walked over and gently placed my hands on her shoulders. She flinched as I leaned in close enough to whisper: "Because there's no one else."

An openly weeping Band-Aid didn't resist as I took her by the hand and led her into the group of helpless heroes. She left them paralyzed. I could've ripped her power and freed them myself. Frankly, I liked them better this way—quiet and helpless.

As for what to do next . . .

I started to laugh as a new plan formed in my head.

"What?" Band-Aid sniffled as she wiped her tears.

I merely shook my head and teleported us all away.

We appeared behind my building, right next to Harlot's capture team. Band-Aid looked around and then gave the downed Triad shooters a curious psychic once-over. The paralyzed heroes looked up at me with varying levels of hope in their eyes. Having heard our conversation, they were happy not to be in the Povchenkos' hands. Still, they didn't know what I had in mind for them.

To be honest, neither did I.

I glanced over at Lia. The acid bomb's residue had burned through enough of the cocoon that I could see her under the alley's harsh lighting. Her forcefield armor was still up, masking her features. I'll have to figure out how to turn it off (so I could salvage it). Something told me that she had more high-end gadgetry lying around. Having had five months to scheme behind everyone's back (including mine), I was a bit curious about Lia's schemes.

Whatever they were, I'd have to tear them down.

"They look like they've been through a screecher," the healer knowingly smiled as she stepped toward the capture team.

"Maybe," I grinned back with a glance at my watch. "Keep 'em comatose while you heal their injuries."

"On it," Band-Aid replied.

I knelt down beside Gratte and patted him down. Sure enough, he had two cigars stashed within his uniform. I stole one and put it in my mouth.

"I thought it was against the regs to smoke during field ops," I muttered.

Gratte angrily groaned in reply. I cleared my throat to get Band-Aid's attention. The healer regarded her former boss for a moment, and then nodded.

"What are you up to, Cly?!" Gratte bellowed as I lit up.

The others thought Band-Aid had undone her paralysis thing, tried to move, and were still barely able to twitch. At least they could talk.

"We get it, Cly! You're not a threat," Glue griped. "Now let us up!"

"In a minute," I replied, savoring the cigar's fine taste. "I'm fighting crime right now."

The ArgoKnights forced themselves to look brave, even though their expressions practically begged for mercy. It was glorious. Lou rushed out and took in the scene.

"Should I even ask, Mr. Cly?" he uttered with a slight shake of the head.

"It's been a long night, Lou," I replied as I stood up and beckoned him over with my right hand. He approached and I casually put my left arm around his neck.

"Lou," I told him, "you're about to finally see some action tonight."

"Really?" he half-grinned.

I nodded and pointed at a large, shadowy part of my building's wall. I opened a shadow portal to the rooftop of a high-rise in Uptown. It gave us a decent view of the abandoned eight-story building I was meaning to hit later.

"This building is in Uptown," I began with a conversational tone. "Kill everyone inside and reduce said building to rubble."

Lou intently studied the structure, which looked vacant and had a large number of "homeless" guys lounging around the perimeter—just like undercover sentries would. None of the windows were lit from within, which implied holograms or a purely sub-level base.

"The targets?" Lou asked.

"High-end mercs would be my guess," I replied. "They just massacred an ArgoKnight training facility. Also, they bribed a bunch of cops to rape poor Pinpoint here."

The Sicilian distastefully frowned as he noticed Pinpoint's unhealed, mostly-naked body. Seeing as he had a daughter about her age, the ex-killer's face hardened.

"Why aren't they moving?" Lou frowned at the downed ArgoKnights.

"A moot point," I assured him. "Now, expect supers, drones, defensive weapons, and the kitchen sink to be thrown at you."

"Consider them handled," Lou vowed as he stepped toward the portal.

"Wait."

He stopped and turned my way.

"You're not leading the attack."

Lou eyed the helpless ArgoKnights with mild scorn.

"You're sending them in first?" he scoffed.

"No," I nodded toward Harlot's guys. "I'm sending your pals."

Lou stiffened, realizing that I had pieced things together. His eyes narrowed as I casually walked over to Harlot's capture team. I had a prime opportunity to see how many powers I could rip . . . and what would happen if I surpassed my limits. At present, I had teleportation, shrinking, tunneling, and Glue's adhesion field. If my augmentation started to fail (again), I'd die. Fortunately, Band-Aid could save me—if she chose to.

"What gave me away?" Lou nervously asked as I ripped the goon with the knowledge absorption power (again). That brought me up to five.

"That would be telling," I replied with a smirk over my left shoulder.

Lou could tear me in half or burn me with his eye beams. Of course, my failsafe would kill him before he could even try. I let him see my lack of fear, which really made him nervous. He assessed the downed ArgoKnights and Band-Aid for a moment.

"This wasn't about money, Mr. Cly," Lou explained. "Harlot threatened my family."

"I know," I patiently smiled as I ripped another Triad guy's copying power away. A nifty little ability, it would let me copy any inanimate object I could lift. Shooters loved this power because they could copy their loaded guns and then shoot all damned day. The duplicate object would be just as real as the original, until X number of hours passed. Then it would turn to dust.

I flinched as Anywhere's teleportation ability went away. The other powers held steady, though. Guess I could only hold five powers at a time. On the sixth, I'd lose the oldest one.

"Fuck," I muttered under my breath, as I glared up at Lou. "You're gonna make amends, Lou. I'm even gonna get you out from under Harlot's thumb."

"How, Mr. Cly?"

The poor guy was both scared and hopeful at the same time. Too bad I couldn't go easy on Lou. In the long run, I was going to get him killed.

"Harlot's got two kids," I hinted. "Did you know that?"

The retired assassin's mouth twisted into a knowing smile as he shook his head.

"You wouldn't happen to have information on them, would you?" Lou asked.

"I'll send you a file," I promised as I ripped an illusion power away from another guy.

There went Speck's shrinking power. My other rips were still good.

This illusion ability was a bit second-rate. The best illusions occurred within a victim's mind; the kind where the targets sensed whatever you wanted them to, through all five senses. This guy's power, however, was merely audio-visual. In essence, I could make temporary holograms that required mild concentration to maintain. Ah well. I could have fun with it.

Let's see . . . the weapons savant was a good one. As long as I had this power, I'd be able to use any weapon with god-like ease. After I ripped the savant, I eyed their healer . . . and then stopped. Nowhere near as good as Band-Aid, this guy simply touched people and allowed their bodies to heal inside of a few minutes. If I ripped it, I'd lose Glue's adhesion power.

I glanced at Glue and decided to keep his power for a bit longer. Then I power gazed the ArgoKnights. They had their powers back (except for Glue) but couldn't use them. Band-Aid had wisely left them just as helpless as when I found them. I liked the way Band-Aid handled herself. I stood up as Lou impatiently waited for my permission to level the building.

"Band-Aid," I nodded toward the Triad shooters. "Wake 'em up on my signal."

"Where are you gonna send them?" she asked. "Inside or outside of the building?"

Good question. I paused for a moment, and then regarded Pinpoint.

"Where'd you stick 'em?" I asked.

Surprised to be consulted, Pinpoint glanced over at Harlot's guys and then the building.

"Grab some goggles," she replied.

"Clever girl," I grinned as I reached down and plucked Gunrack's pair off her face.

"These won't flash-bang me, will they?" I joked as I took her goggles and slipped them on.

"No," Gunrack replied, more than cool with idea of me killing these motherfuckers.

Too bad we weren't alone. The idea of having her here (all helpless) distracted me for a moment. Gunrack noticed that lusty gleam in my eye . . .

Then I turned away and scanned the building.

"Come on! Come on!" I muttered under my breath. "Papa needs a nice fucking bullseye."

While the structure was protected by some kind of jamming field, it wasn't ArgoKnight-grade. The sensors revealed personnel on seven floors and three sub-levels. The servers were on the fifth floor. The command level appeared to be on the fourth. The top floor was a vacant buffer zone, layered with booby traps. It was a clever precaution to take against rooftop insertions.

I grinned as I turned toward Anywhere.

"Put 'em on the roof, please."

"Okaaay," the teleporter replied as Band-Aid allowed him to move again.

Anywhere stood up, decided to play nice this time, and then studied the rooftop for a moment. He then stepped amongst Harlot's guys.

"Now?" Band-Aid asked.

I gave her the nod.

The capture team suddenly began to stir. Then, with an implosion of air, Anywhere took the fuckers off my hands. I adjusted the shadow tunnel and gave them a close-up view of the Triad guys via a rooftop shadow. All eyes turned toward the rooftop as Anywhere brought them in and then quickly teleported away. The Triad goons came to, looked around, and then hastily grabbed their guns. Some of them rushed over to the roof's edges and covered each side of the building.

Unsure of how they got here, the shooters radioed in.

A half-second later, hidden spotlights shined throughout the exterior. On the ground level, the "winos" jumped to their feet with assault rifles at the ready. They turned their guns upwards and immediately opened fire on the rooftop. Harlot's goons returned fire.

Bodies began to fall on both sides.

"Nice," I grinned, pleased that someone (other than me) was tiptoeing into that shitstorm.

"What about the servers?" Diglet asked. "They might be wiping them as we speak."

"Good point," I sighed as I shifted the shadow tunnel to the server room.

Three skinny techs scrambled around in dark slacks and matching white shirts. In the background was a complex server array. Alarms sounded off with a deafening whine as I hopped into the shallow tunnel and exited from the shadow of a supply cabinet. As I quietly fell into the server room, I tapped my holstered Colt with both hands. With a grin, I now had two duplicate Colts in my hands.

Since none of the techs had spotted me (yet), I took in my surroundings.

The rectangular room took up the entire floor with servers lining the walls. I brushed up against one of the vending machine-sized devices. Like the others, it was plugged into everything. I kicked on the knowledge absorption power and—

Diglet was right. They were wiping the servers. Fuck! I barely managed to grab seventeen percent of their files. The rest was reduced to digital ashes. I gazed the techs over and wasn't too surprised to see that they were all psi-hackers. They were so distracted with wiping the server files that they hadn't noticed me yet.

My Colts came with built-in tasers in the butts, which I had never used. Now, as I jumped across the room, I had an excuse. The nearest psi-hacker yelped as he heard me land behind him. I reversed the grip on my right-handed Colt and tased him in the balls. The poor geek hit the floor in convulsing unconsciousness.

I stepped on him and ripped his power as I aimed the other Colt at his pals, who both gawked at me.

"Hiya, fellas."

The pair of unarmed geeks drew back in fear as I kicked on the weapons savant ability. One look at my evil smile told them to flee, which they did. I gave them a running head start before gunning them down with Embedder rounds. Then I walked away and let them explode. The blasts shredded the other side of the level. Debris and smoke harmlessly flew past me as I reached the closet and then half-stepped into its shadow.

Then I emptied both six-shooters into every (remaining) support column in the room. Judging from the not-so-random dispersal of my gunfire, the explosions might actually collapse the fifth floor. I dropped the Colts and fell through a newly made shadow tunnel, which put me right back into the alley. I rolled to my feet and sealed it right as the server room blew.

"Well! That was fun," I smiled.

Band-Aid politely applauded as Anywhere reappeared with an armful of street clothes for himself and his lady.

"Um . . . can you let her up?" Anywhere meekly asked.

I looked over at Band-Aid and gave her the nod. "Heal her up too, eh?"

Pinpoint winced as her shoulder relocated. Then she sighed with relief as her visible injuries faded away.

"Thanks," she said to me.

Able to move, the other ArgoKnights slowly stood up. Band-Aid watched them like a gunslinger, almost daring them to try anything. Pinpoint rushed over and gave Anywhere an enviable French kiss. As the lovers divvied up their clothes and started to get dressed, the other ArgoKnights eyed me with a mix of awe and disapproval.

"Did you have to shoot those guys?" Glue asked.

"Probably," I replied.

"But you trashed the servers!" Speck scolded me. "We don't even know who these buggers are working for."

I had a fair amount of useful data in my head. Names, missions, and even bank accounts were at my psychic fingertips. However, any files on the *Status Quo's* leadership and core mission had been wiped clean. When this was over, I'd have to meet with Reckoner and compare notes.

"The techs were all psi-hackers," I innocently shrugged. "Judging from the building's heavy reliance on automated weapons, both the servers and the psi-hackers had to go. Sorry."

My argument was logical (even true). The shrinker shook her head as Lou tossed his doorman's hat to the ground.

"Shall I be off, Mr. Cly?" Lou asked.

"Yeah, Lou," I replied, offering my hand. "Thanks for everything."

After a moment's hesitation, the Sicilian shook it. Before I let go, I gently pulled him in.

"As for your amends," I said with quiet menace, "you're moving to Canada—as in right after this last job. Don't even pack."

Lou blinked with relief, not minding the idea of being closer to his family.

"You don't work for me or anyone else," I continued. "Your severance package will be wired to our agreed-upon account. Security arrangements, for your family, are on you."

Lou nodded, waiting for the other shoe to drop.

"In exchange for my not ripping out your fucking throat," I sighed, "you will fight crime."

"In Canada?" he frowned.

"It should be dull," I nodded. "Still, I expect to read about your exploits. Also, within a year, I want to hear about a team of Canadian super heroes called *The Doormen*. Set up your own lairs, intel sources, logistics, members, and so on. Do it how you see fit. If you need help, I'm but a phone call away."

"Understood, Mr. Cly," Lou nodded apparently intrigued by the idea.

I let him go.

"One last thing," I said as I backed away. "My daughter's dead. Harlot's partially to blame for that . . . and so are you."

That last part was probably bullshit. Knowing *Status Quo*, they could've just popped an inhibitor pulse and then rushed in shooting. They didn't really need to scout out my security. Still, in Lia's fucked-up future, it was possible that Harlot sold them the intel in the first place.

"What?! Lia's dead?" Lou followed my gaze toward Lia and his jaw dropped.

While he had noticed the cocooned corpse, the translucent forcefield concealed her features. The Sicilian took a step toward her and then stopped. We could all see the intense shame on his face as he angrily cursed in his native tongue.

Lou had genuinely liked Lia. Respected her.

"I-I'm so sorry!" Lou gasped as his eyes glowed red. "I didn't know, Mr. Cly! *I didn't know!*"

"Take it out on the building," I grimly replied.

Full of regret and rage, Lou nodded and took to the sky so fast that my clothes billowed in his wake.

CHAPTER TWENTY

I watched Gunrack through the shadows of the *Shattered Deuce.*

Dressed in beige khakis, black Lugz boots, and a white t-shirt, she looked very much at home here. Her crucifix was under the t-shirt as she finished a teardrop tattoo on some white thug with cornrows. Gunrack's tattoo parlor was a 24/7 establishment which catered to all sorts—from surly bikers to drunk college kids out to "get cut" together. Covered with samples of her art, it was clear to see that the gal had talent.

Just past midnight, Karl sat behind the counter with a copy of *Sports Illustrated.* In his late 40's, the skinny, bald Support Staffer was covered with tats and uglier than me. He ran the shop whenever Gunrack was out on "official" business. Something of a dick, Karl never had much to say to me. At a glance, he lacked any obvious powers. But after the last few days' worth of mayhem, I'm sure he was packing a small arsenal.

Gunrack took the thug's money, watched him leave, and then gawked as I climbed out of the shadow of her front entrance. Karl dropped the magazine and pulled a sawed-down Ithaca pump from behind the counter. The shotgun's barrel gave off a soft, ominous whine as I rose to my feet. My ex merely slid her hands into her deep pockets, probably ready to draw a pair of guns—if need be.

"Hi," I scowled as I wiped dirt off my hands.

"You're early, Cly," Gunrack said with a tense smile. "I thought you weren't gonna kill me for another hour."

"More like fifty-seven minutes," I sighed as I eased my way over to a burnt-orange waiting couch and plopped down. "And I'm just taking a break. Thought I'd spend it with you."

Karl had a clear line of fire. Even with his fancy weapon, I ignored him. He wouldn't shoot unless Gunrack gave him the signal. Should it come to that, I'd end them both.

"What's it like out there?" she asked.

"Quiet," I lied.

Over the last few hours, I stopped four muggings, a jewel heist, some attempted murders, and a trio of idiots trying to lace City Hall with thermobaric charges.

Gunrack's smile eased up a bit. "We both know you're not gonna kill me if I stay."

My eyes narrowed.

"If I can kill my daughter, I can sure as fuck kill you. Sit down."

Gunrack swallowed hard as she realized I was in a killer's mood. Then she carefully pulled her hands from her pockets and then sat in the nearest tattoo chair. I crossed my legs and got down to business.

"I have a few questions about Malcolm O'Flernan."

Her eyes narrowed at the mention of his name. "What kind of questions?"

"Even though his dad's out of the picture, I might still have to kill the boy . . . *Vivian*."

Gunrack (a.k.a., Vivian Hallett) gave me a rueful sigh as she looked over at Karl.

"Take a break," she told him with a nod toward the front window.

Karl reluctantly set the weapon down behind the counter. He slipped on a jacket and gave me a glare of warning on the way out.

"What gave me away?" she asked.

"You tapped into your psi-link while Teke was working on Malcolm's psyche," I replied with an understanding smile.

"I had to know my son was all right," Gunrack sighed. "I figured Teke wouldn't notice."

"You thought wrong," I replied with a smug grin. "Now, let's step back to the beginning. Why were you fucking around with Seamus' boys anyway?"

"My mission was to infiltrate the O'Flernan clan and study their operations. Both brothers took a liking to me, so I played them."

Her expression softened. "Connor was a good lay. Angus was a good man."

"Seamus ordered Harlan to kill his own sons, didn't he?"

Vivian nodded, curious as to how I knew any of this.

"Seamus decided to kill his own sons when Malcolm was born," Vivian explained with a hint of disgust.

"But why would he?" I asked.

"Seamus was a big-picture kind of bastard," Vivian explained. "In his eyes, Connor would've been a decent Shepherd but never a boss. Angus actually wanted to go legit, which would've made him look weak and . . ."

". . . . gotten him killed," I finished.

The Section Chief's face fell. I think she really liked Angus (maybe even more than she did me).

"As much as the old man loved his sons," she bitterly added, "Seamus O'Flernan loved his empire more. Keeping that legacy going meant more to him than his own flesh-and-blood."

"Either one could've been psi-trained like Deidre was," I argued.

"Seamus didn't believe in that shit," Vivian scoffed as she pulled out a pack of Newports.

She offered me one. I declined with a polite shake of my head.

"He wanted an heir who had the innate mettle to take the reins."

"Why didn't you just take Malcolm and run?" I asked.

"I was supposed to be an ambitious corporate viper that hated kids," Vivian replied as she lit up. "Seamus offered me a valued place in the organization if I gave him Malcolm. So I did, knowing that my son would grow up in a safe, secure home—something I couldn't give him."

Her expression revealed both her sadness and self-loathing. Such was the price of being a good soldier. Still, it was the smart move. Even if Vivian had successfully managed to kidnap her son, Seamus would've hunted them to the ends of the Earth and then killed her. Even if she could've raised him, life as a Section Chief's only son wasn't exactly safer.

"How'd your mission go?" I asked.

"I earned their trust and had eyes on their international ops for the next ten years," Vivian shrugged with a hint of pride. "My work saved a lot of lives. Then came *Clean Sweep.*"

Her face soured.

"Somewhere along the line, my cover was blown and I had to switch identities."

During those dark weeks, she had to choose between rescuing her son and saving as many ArgoKnights as she could. While Vivian made the right call, it was a hard one. No wonder they made her a Section Chief. The gal put the cause first and foremost.

"Why didn't you leave your son in Malibu?"

Vivian exhaled a plume of smoke.

"Last year, I learned that Malcolm's adopted parents were starting to groom him to run the mob," she scowled. "I couldn't justify a standard rescue op. So I had Seamus O'Flernan killed."

That made me blink.

"What are you talking about?" I balked. "Pinpoint killed him on my order . . . *oh you sly bitch!* You ordered her to take him out!"

Vivian shook her head with a slight grin.

"Pinpoint was Plan B. Remember the serving girl?"

On the rooftop of the *Versantio Hotel*, where the shooting happened, Seamus met me after finishing dinner. He had three feds (posing as bodyguards) walk me up. There was a blonde serving gal who I could never track down. When his bodyguards attacked me, she up and disappeared without a fucking trace.

"A Support Staffer?"

"A freelancer," Gunrack corrected me. "She poisoned his cigar. Had Seamus survived his meeting with you, the old man would've died in his sleep."

"Then you'd have had it written off as natural causes, eh?" I nodded.

"I expected my son to get lost in the shuffle," she sighed. "That's why I tasked Glue to bring him here, to me. Someone tried to stop him."

More than likely it was my late daughter.

"You'd have made a good mom," I said.

Vivian studied me as she put her lighter away, slowly rose, and gestured for me to follow.

"So what about my son?" she nervously asked as we headed into the back room.

"I'm on the fence," I replied. "You carried Malcolm in your womb for nine months. Your psi-link's stronger than his dad's. Letting someone that dangerous live is a big fucking mistake."

"Do that and I'll kill you," she vowed without slowing her stride.

There were parlor supplies, four narrow metal lockers, and a taped-up punching bag. At the other end was a narrow flight of darkened stairs. Gunrack paused to leave her cigarette in a small plastic ashtray. Then she led me downstairs.

Even though I believed Gunrack's threat, I had to chuckle.

"What?" she asked, mildly offended by my reaction.

"I can't believe that Glue played me," I grinned. "All that bullshit about Seamus hiring him to kidnap Malcolm. Maybe he's not so second-rate after all."

"He's one of my best," she nodded.

"Why risk the kid's life at all?" I asked. "Anywhere could've whisked the kid away years ago."

"Seeing as Anywhere was on your payroll, Seamus would've killed you," she replied. "As much as we didn't like you, Cly, your firm was important."

I thought back to the part where Pinpoint gloated about running ArgoKnight ops through my firm. Never thought I'd live to see them reduced to outsourcing their justice.

"The best I could do," Gunrack continued, "was leave him some money and op tech, and then let it play out. Someone got wind of the mission and gave Glue a rough time."

"You ID those responsible?"

"Not yet," Gunrack assured me, "but we will. When Glue got to Pillar City, I steered him toward you, knowing that if he left Malcolm with you . . ."

". . . that I'd protect him long enough to hand him over to you fuckers," I finished. "Clever plan. Too bad Connor was slumming in his son's mind."

We reached the bottom of the stairs.

"Is that why you had him collared?"

She merely turned and met my gaze. I grinned, wondering what she wasn't telling me.

"The thing is, Vivian, you two can still blow up the fucking world—or take it over."

Gunrack thoughtfully closed her eyes for a moment.

"I can't psi-link with him now," she admitted.

"Teke's handiwork?"

"Doesn't mean it can't be undone," I replied. "You know this."

The ArgoKnight tensely bit her lower lip, deep in thought.

"What do you want, Cly?"

"Get out of my city within the next hour," I replied. "The kid goes elsewhere. Don't look for him. Don't try to recruit him. I'll see to his safety."

Vivian stared at me with intense frustration. Couldn't blame her. She wanted nothing more than to raise her only child (too bad Fate kept getting in the way).

"And you'll really kill me if I'm here past 1 a.m.? Or if I ever come back?"

"With more regret than pleasure," I straight up told her.

Gunrack paused to size up the angles of an abrupt departure.

"Who's gonna supply you?"

"I can find anything in this town," I replied with a wink. "It'll just cost more."

I didn't mention the dozens upon dozens of *Status Quo* accounts I had psi-hacked last night. With the scant amount of intel I managed to steal, I siphoned off about $415 million in liquid assets. The missions they've pulled suggested that this figure was little more than "petty cash" to them. Worse, these guys had more manpower and resources than I ever did as a fixer.

With a frustrated sigh, Gunrack continued onward. The small basement was something of a private gallery. Her signature was on every piece. The shit was so good that I had even bought a few. Tucked in secure vaults, I knew they'd be worth a fortune someday. I noticed some new paintings on her walls (ones I hadn't seen yet).

Gunrack impatiently waited as I stopped to admire them.

"A shame this is only a hobby for you," I mused as I eyed a picture of a pinkish-gray storm cloud caught in the sun's haunting rays. It was drawn so realistically it could've been a photo.

"Art keeps me sane," Gunrack replied.

I followed her to the circular platform. To the uninitiated, it looked like a floor mural. Surrounded by white linoleum flooring, the abstract mural was a mixture of metals set in swirling patterns. At her approach, the mural spiraled open to reveal a concealed platform.

"I'm sorry it ended like this," Gunrack said with an impish smile. "You're the best ex I've ever had."

"At least you get to live," I replied, thinking of Lia.

Gunrack caught my meaning as we stepped on the platform, within easy kissing range (something we used to often do when riding this thing).

"You're being too hard on yourself," she said with open sympathy.

"Lia's dead because of me," I reminded her. "The appropriate response would be to put a gun in my mouth."

Gunrack awkwardly looked away as she snapped her fingers. The platform quickly and smoothly descended into a dimly lit, ovular lab. Motion-activated lighting flickered on overhead as we entered. Lined with crimson metal walls and all kinds of interesting weaponry, the space lacked the clutter of a typical weapons lab. While it looked Spartanesque, Gunrack's workshop was actually concealed within the walls, floors, and ceiling.

There was an old black La-Z-Boy recliner near the center of the room. To the right of it was a small table with a stack of sketchpads and sharpened pencils. To the left was a brown mini-fridge with a half-empty bottle of beer on top of it. This was where Gunrack did her best thinking. Once she started dating me, we did quite a few interesting things in that chair . . .

"I could use a beer—if it's not poisoned, that is."

"Now you're talkin'," she smiled.

The ex-soldier crouched at the fridge, giving me a quaint view of her plump ass. As she did, I gazed her powers for the first time. When we met, Gunrack told me that she was simply a super genius. During our time together, she never gave me any cause to suspect otherwise until Connor mentioned his kid's mom being a psychic. Then there was her son's Omega-level psi-link. So, naturally, I had to take a gander . . .

What I saw left my head spinning.

Her genius ability was natural-born, as well as her innate affinity with warfare. If I had to guess, Gunrack came from a family of super soldiers. As a psychic, she could learn the skills of anyone she met (like me). Cooler still, she could pass them on to anyone who let her. Right now, she's probably got hundreds—maybe thousands—of individual skill sets buzzing around in her head.

Gunrack could've been the ultimate psi-trainer and that alone would've impressed me.

What gave me a boner (aside from her perfect ass) was that she could create weapons *out of thin-fucking air*! An incredibly rare form of psychic creation, Gunrack could think of any hand-held weapon and make it permanently appear—as long as she knew how it worked.

Of course, the sly killer was already smart enough to design her own toys. Add to that her role as a weapons tester. Other geniuses not only gave her their weapons (and schematics) to review, their skills might get copied if they physically met with her. With a mind like hers, Gunrack could create thousands of different weapons and gadgets on the fly.

If she wasn't the most dangerous woman on Earth, Gunrack had to be in the top-fucking-ten. No wonder Malcolm had a Mark-10 collar around his neck. Vivian was afraid that if his powers manifested (during his abduction), they might become uncontrollable.

I kept my expression even as she turned my way.

"So, what happened when you met with Harlot?" Gunrack asked as she tossed me a beer. "About that pimp?"

I forced out a laugh as I popped the bottle cap.

"The bitch actually canceled on me!"

"What?!" Gunrack laughed. "You're kidding!"

I shook my head and took a swig of the delicious brew. Her taste in micro-brewed beers rivaled her talent in art.

"Apparently, some bad man had her elite capture team stranded atop a building of heavily-armed mercs. Then, while they were busy killing each other, a small Sicilian guy (dressed as a doorman) swooped down and leveled the place. A bunch of Wung gunships showed up and got burned out of the sky by said Sicilian."

"We should've left a camera or two to record the fight," Gunrack grinned as she sat in her recliner and crossed her legs Indian-style. "Fox News reported that it was a 'movie shoot' for an upcoming action flick."

They would. I shook my head with amused disgust.

"A year ago, under different circumstances, the Wungs would've hired me to clean this up," I said with a wince. "Spin control's not really their thing."

"So that's why Harlot canceled on you? She's too busy bribing this away?"

"Partially," I replied, pausing a moment to take a swig, "I also think Harlot's a bit scared of me . . . and she should be."

"It isn't over, you know," Gunrack warned me. "Harlot's not the type to forgive and forget."

I gave my ex a scary, eager smile.

"I know."

"By the way, Grace is awake," Gunrack said, changing the subject.

"How is she?" I asked, hoping for some good news.

"Band-Aid's got her at 100% and I've removed her implants for repair. Only, her psi-hacking doesn't work anymore."

"The psi-hacking's a latent power," I realized, after a moment's pause. "Without the instability in her head, Grace can't tap it?"

Gunrack nodded, a bit surprised that I pieced it together so fast.

"Sucks to be her," I sighed. "Talk her out of a psi-hacking augmentation. With all of the bounties on her head, Grace should pick something dangerous."

"I'll do that," the ArgoKnight replied with an approving smile as she sipped her beer. "You really should've joined us, Cly."

"Don't insult me," I replied, meeting her gaze for a few seconds. "Speaking of the ArgoKnights, how are they recovering?"

Gunrack gave me a teasing frown.

"ArgoKnights? They're a long-dead hero team—or haven't you heard?"

"My mistake," I played along. "Guess I'll never see them out in the open again, eh?"

"Damned right you won't," she assured me.

I began to pace around her backside.

"Hopefully, there's someone out there to warn me of impending threats to the world."

"Count on it," Gunrack replied, after another sip. "Based on what you did with Lou, I wouldn't be too surprised if other freelance hero groups come out of the woodwork."

"Really?" I replied with a hopeful grin. "I wonder who'd be crazy enough to supply them with op tech and weaponry?"

"Probably someone who used to live in Pillar City," Gunrack sadly replied. "Someone who missed out on a perfect engagement ring."

We stood there in awkward silence.

"So, why are we down here?"

Gunrack took a long swig from her bottle.

"Lia," she replied with quiet sadness.

I took a deep breath, hoping they didn't fuck me over again. Back in the alley, Gunrack had offered to disable the forcefield armor so I could cremate my kid. When she asked me to debrief her on our psychic encounter, I was too tired to distrust her. Besides, I had to talk to someone.

So I told the ArgoKnights what happened—everything. Then I let them take her away. Speck shrank the cocoon to the size of a pocket comb and Anywhere teleported them to this lab. I stayed put, hit the shower, and got ready for my dawn meeting with Harlot. When that fell through, I merely went to bed and slept until nightfall.

"Where is she?" I asked.

"Open Vault 3," Gunrack commanded.

A section of the ceiling slid open and a stasis vault smoothly emerged. The circular construct was lined in both red metal and patches of transparent plastic. As long as the stasis vault was active, time would practically freeze around her. Lit from the inside with a bluish light, we could see Lia's corpse inside. She looked so damned peaceful . . .

"It took me a few hours to disable the armor," she explained. "Good shit, too."

"Can you salvage it?" I asked.

"Yeah," Gunrack nodded as she moved behind me. "You want the specs?"

I nodded. The badge's mechanism had shrugged off an inhibitor pulse, which would make it quite useful down the road.

"You might wanna consider upgrading ACHE with it," I advised. "After last night, I've developed a healthy respect for energy forms."

Gunrack pursed her luscious lips for a moment, and then nodded with a quick grin. I knew that look. Within a few months, ACHE would probably be able to kick my ass. Good. In a world this unforgiving, the AI would need to be able to look out for itself.

"Vault 3," she ordered, "viewing position."

The stasis vault slid into a horizontal position, much like a coffin. The lighting turned off as the upper shell slid open. Able to reach out and touch her, I looked down on my daughter's corpse and waited to feel anything. When nothing happened, I simply sipped my beer.

"We're going to have a service for her," Gunrack offered. "A lot of her friends wanted to pay their respects—"

"Burn it," I told her, thinking of the profits one could make by auctioning off my kid's remains.

"Cly," she started to argue.

"Burn. It."

Gunrack sighed, took me by the arm, and gestured for me to step back.

"Vault 3 . . . Disposal Protocol."

Lia's stasis vault sealed itself. Then there was white flash of intense light. While Gunrack averted her eyes, I didn't bother. After a few seconds, all that was left of Lia Falsham were ashes and mixed memories. I finished my beer and gently set it on the fridge. Gunrack did the same.

"Thank you," I muttered as I pulled my mask down and turned to leave.

"Dim lights," Gunrack said.

The overhead lighting flickered and then dimmed around me. Surrounded by shadows, I picked one and opened a shadow tunnel onto a Downtown rooftop. Sounds of traffic and loud rap music came through from the other side.

"What about her ashes?"

"Keep 'em," I replied.

"The funeral," Gunrack sighed, "I'll let you know when and where."

"Don't bother," I told her. "I've just paid my respects."

"I don't understand, Cly," Gunrack said as she followed me toward the shadow tunnel. "You need to take some time off; to grieve."

I turned to face her.

"I've been grieving all night," I told her with a hard edge. "I'm gonna share my grief with every two-bit motherfucker I come across. It's been my experience that it's more cathartic than crying in the dark."

With a sad smile, Gunrack stepped up and gave me a tight hug. After a moment's hesitation, I hugged her back. As much as I wanted to keep Gunrack here or go into hiding with her, I knew better. I had violated my Community Service, which was tantamount to an act of war.

The O'Flernans and the Wungs were able to come at me directly now. The sooner Gunrack left Pillar City, the better . . . especially when she realized what I had in mind. I jumped through the shadows and landed on the rooftop. Hate welled up within me as I looked around the Downtown skyline.

Pillar City used to amuse me.

Now, I fucking hated the place. Had I raised Lia anywhere else, she might be alive right now. In a roundabout way, Pillar City was responsible for my kid's madness and death.

In a similar fashion, I was going to return the favor.

THE END

ABOUT THE AUTHOR

Marcus V. Calvert is a native of Detroit who grew up with an addiction to sci-fi that just wouldn't go away.

His goal's to tell unique, twisted stories that people will be reading long after he's gone. For him, the name and the fame aren't important. Only the stories matter.

You can find his books on Amazon and/or follow him on Facebook.

His website is: **https://squareup.com/store/TANSOM.**